Acting Edition

AF278354

I Wanna Fuck Like Romeo and Juliet

by Andrew Rincón

Copyright © 2023 by Andrew Rincón
All Rights Reserved

I WANNA FUCK LIKE ROMEO AND JULIET is fully protected under the copyright laws of the United States of America, the British Commonwealth, including Canada, and all member countries of the Berne Convention for the Protection of Literary and Artistic Works, the Universal Copyright Convention, and/or the World Trade Organization conforming to the Agreement on Trade Related Aspects of Intellectual Property Rights. All rights, including professional and amateur stage productions, recitation, lecturing, public reading, motion picture, radio broadcasting, television, online/digital production, and the rights of translation into foreign languages are strictly reserved.

ISBN 978-0-573-71032-2

www.concordtheatricals.com
www.concordtheatricals.co.uk

FOR PRODUCTION INQUIRIES

UNITED STATES AND CANADA
info@concordtheatricals.com
1-866-979-0447

UNITED KINGDOM AND EUROPE
licensing@concordtheatricals.co.uk
020-7054-7298

Each title is subject to availability from Concord Theatricals Corp., depending upon country of performance. Please be aware that *I WANNA FUCK LIKE ROMEO AND JULIET* may not be licensed by Concord Theatricals Corp. in your territory. Professional and amateur producers should contact the nearest Concord Theatricals Corp. office or licensing partner to verify availability.

CAUTION: Professional and amateur producers are hereby warned that *I WANNA FUCK LIKE ROMEO AND JULIET* is subject to a licensing fee. The purchase, renting, lending or use of this book does not constitute a license to perform this title(s), which license must be obtained from Concord Theatricals Corp. prior to any performance. Performance of this title(s) without a license is a violation of federal law and may subject the producer and/or presenter of such performances to civil penalties. Both amateurs and professionals considering a production are strongly advised to apply to the appropriate agent before starting rehearsals, advertising, or booking a theatre. A licensing fee must be paid whether the title(s) is presented for charity or gain and whether or not admission is charged. Professional/Stock licensing fees are quoted upon application to Concord Theatricals Corp.

This work is published by Samuel French, an imprint of Concord Theatricals Corp.

No one shall make any changes in this title(s) for the purpose of production. No part of this book may be reproduced, stored in a retrieval system, scanned, uploaded, or transmitted in any form, by any means, now known or yet to be invented, including mechanical, electronic, digital, photocopying, recording, videotaping, or otherwise, without the prior written permission of the publisher. No one shall share this title(s), or any part of this title(s), through any social media or file hosting websites.

For all inquiries regarding motion picture, television, online/digital and other media rights, please contact Concord Theatricals Corp.

MUSIC AND THIRD-PARTY MATERIALS USE NOTE

Licensees are solely responsible for obtaining formal written permission from copyright owners to use copyrighted music and/or other copyrighted third-party materials (e.g. artworks, logos) in the performance of this play and are strongly cautioned to do so. If no such permission is obtained by the licensee, then the licensee must use only original music and materials that the licensee owns and controls. Licensees are solely responsible and liable for clearances of all third-party copyrighted materials, including without limitation music, and shall indemnify the copyright owners of the play(s) and their licensing agent, Concord Theatricals Corp., against any costs, expenses, losses and liabilities arising from the use of such copyrighted third-party materials by licensees. For music, please contact the appropriate music licensing authority in your territory for the rights to any incidental music.

IMPORTANT BILLING AND CREDIT REQUIREMENTS

If you have obtained performance rights to this title, please refer to your licensing agreement for important billing and credit requirements.

I WANNA FUCK LIKE ROMEO AND JULIET was first produced by Michael Aguirre, of the New Light Theater Project (Sarah Norris, Founding Artistic Director, Michael Aguirre, Founding Producing Director) at 59e59 Theaters in New York City on October 20, 2022. The Artistic Producer was William Steinberger. The performance was directed by Jesse Jou, with intimacy and fight choreography by Denise A. Hurd. Scenic design was by Brittany Vasta, costume design was by Antonio Consuegra, lighting design was by Annie Wiegand, sound design was by Margaret Montagna, and props were by Jenna Arkontaky. The Production Stage Manager was B. Rafidi, the Assistant Stage Manager was Kyle S. Ronyecs, and the Production Assistant was Sommer Schaap. Casting was by Gama Valle. The cast was as follows:

CUPID	Jacqueline Guillén
VALENTINE	Greg Cuellar
BENNY RANDLE	Ashton Muñiz
ALEJANDRO DIAZ	Juan Arturo
BETTI	Elizabeth Ramos
THE POET	The Company

An early version of this play was presented at Pork Filled Productions, Seattle, WA, 2019.

CHARACTERS

The Gods

CUPID – God of Love. Appears as a Latiné woman in her twenties to thirties. Puts on a bitter, hard exterior. Incredibly heartbroken and tired. Fierce and Ferocious. Speaks Spanish and English.

VALENTINE – Patron Saint of Love. Appears as any ethnicity, slightly younger than Cupid. Joyous, a rascal – more of a trickster than a saint. Believer in Love, completely and indefinitely.

THE POET – God, or something like it. A voice. Also voices **ALEXA**, **SCRUFF VOICES** and **REPORTER**.

The Lovers

BENNY RANDLE – Mid-twenties Black Queer Man. Avoids the difficult questions by putting on a façade of ridiculousness and fabulousness. Lover to Alejandro. Mortal.

ALEJANDRO DIAZ – Mid-thirties Latiné Queer Man. Runs from anything that can hurt him. Sedate and steady like water, and just as stubborn. Lover to Benny. Mortal. Speaks Spanish and English.

The Dental Hygeinist

BETTI – A Woman of Color. A child of immigrants and a dental hygienist. In her thirties. Incredibly sad, incredibly eager. Looking for something new in her life. Mortal, with untapped potential for the Divine.

SETTING

The Celestial Heavens (located in outer space).
Hackensack, NJ (various locations).
A World of Canyons.
A World of Ocean.

TIME

Present day.

AUTHOR'S NOTE

A "/" or "//" indicates overlapping dialogue between two characters.

Quick Note on The Poet

There is flexibility around The Poet. It can be voiced by another actor in the ensemble (if you do this, please make the voice distinct from the other character). Or The Poet's lines can be divided among multiple actors, but beware that the line between confusing and clear is thin. I always imagine The Poet's voice to be one voice that is more femme and queer coded, and I always hear it on a god mic in my head. But do whatever is best for your production and its design.

Para Mami – la Guerrera con un corazón más grande que los cielos

For Queer Folx who keep on planting Queer Love in the World.

And for D. Thank you for showing me a Great Love. Capital Everything.

ACT ONE

Scene One

(Darkness.)

(A voice is heard.)

THE POET. Hey!

It's nice to see you!

Sorry I'm over here? I guess that's bad directional-a-torily? (Is that a word?)

I don't have a body so I'm like, you know, all around you. And in you. *(Embarrassed.)* I just meant that I'm in every little thing...molecule...or whatever...

(A beat as the voice sighs.)

I'm bad at this. I mean part of my whole "job," for lack of a better word, is NOT talking about myself. Let's start over. Backspace, Backspace, Backspace. It might help to give you something to look at...

(On stage lights glow. They look like the Northern Lights – hundreds of colors meld into a lightshow that lives and breathes.)

(It's soft and lovely.)

(The voice takes a seriously epic tone.)

THE POET.   Some call me Him. Or Her. Or They. Some call me Dios. The Alpha and The Omega. I am Elohim and Allah. I am the Holy Unknown, the Orishas and Oshun, Jeovah, I'm the Spiritual Force and Creatrix of the Universe. I'm that Feeling you get when you find a twenty dollar bill in a pair of jeans, *and* I'm the hateful fist that broke your jaw. I'm your mind when it goes white with orgasm, and *sometimes* – I'm nothing at all.

(A long beat.)

(Campy.) Hiiiiiiiiiiiiiiiiiiiiiiiiiiiiiiiiiiiiiiiiiiiiiiiiiiiiiiiiiii.

To be honest I hate the term "God". It's limiting and a bit too "fe fi fo fum." I'm more of an Artist? A Poet. Everything, everyone is a bit of a poem. Some really bad. Some really good (not to brag).

But poems – either way.

No one that I know of has called me the Poet, mind you. So feel free to go out in the world and spread that around. Or not. I'll love you either way! I love everything! All. The. Time.

Except Rivers. Rivers are assholes. I love them too of course, it's just the WAY they talk to you sometimes. They're rude in that passive aggressive office coworker type of way.

Yes, yes, they are drying up and I should be more empathetic... I'm trying.

(We hear a snap.)

(Lights shift – to the darkness of space. Lights blink on and off like stars.)

Welcome, my little Poems, to a story about...

(A quick pause as **THE POET** *thinks.)*

Hmmm. How to choose, how to choose...

Stories are like delicious spices in a beloved pantry for me.

It's hard to find the right words.

what to call *this*...

Hm.

Hm Hmmm. *(To themselves.)* Bitch figure it out...

How about...

It's about the flavors of love?

Sure – dale, that sounds spicy.

It's a story shaped around the different flavors of love

And it's about Journeys, both spiritual and physical.

Okay that's good I think. I think that's, *(In a Mario-type of voice.)* thass a good descriptor!

> *(Small beat as* **THE POET** *gets embarrassed.)*

Oh *god* I just used my Mario voice.

My friends tell me that's what I sound like when I'm nervous.

Mario...the plumber...Nintendo...

Let me shut up.

> *(She can't.)*

I'm just nervous that I might have not described this right. And I'm nervous because for me...telling a story feels...

Like a love letter?

Like something warm and gentle whispered into your ear.

Whispered by someone you feel safe by.

It's a kiss...when you tell a story...

(**THE POET** *gets serious.*)

THE POET. So? (*Pause.*) Come closer.

Lean in close to me.

(**THE POET** *breathes. Then whispers.*)

We'll start in...Outer Space...

(Uyyy pero I like that!!) Eso, we start in Outer Space. Where the God of love Cupid –

...*yes* I said Cupid.

(Not the version you're thinking of, fat little annoying baby-man shooting people with sticks.)

Esta Diosa, *our* God of Love, is a different type of Cupid.

Una diosa con un poquitito mas...sabór

Con un poco mas Adobó y aguapanela,

This Cupid is a *warrior*

Luchadora, Soldada, Guerrera del Amor, con un berraquera sin comparación en todo los Cielos

So we start with Cupid glaring at Planet Earth.

From a rock in Outer Space...

(**THE POET** *fades out.*)

(*Slowly, falling like a lost petal,* **CUPID** *lands in front of us. She appears as a Latina woman. Casual clothes. A White Tank, jeans. Intricate tattoos over her body.*)

(*Emerging from her back are two wings. They were once beautiful, but are now old, tattered, with feathers limp and missing in patches.*)

(*In her hands is a large shotgun.*)

(She turns to look at Earth in the distance, watching it for a long moment.)

CUPID. ¿Sabes qué? This always felt good. Standing here, wrapped up in the silence and stars, watching you spin slowly like a drunk viejito on the dance floor. Valentine always says that if it wasn't for work, I'd pass away the centuries up here staring at you while I cleaned La Loca.

(She looks at the shotgun in her hands.)

I always loved sneaking up here whenever I could, in between the first kisses, flirty side eyes, one night stands and vows of amor eterno...'Cause let me tell you, this shit right here?

Was Cupid's happy place. Entiendes? A refuge. Mine.

Millenia being this. Being Cupid. Do you know what that's like? Experiencing time not as seconds into minutes, but living life as a million, trillion, little heartbreaks crashing into you *constantly?*

But it's fine. Because I'm the God of Love, La Guerrera, La Luchadora, La Berraca Cupid. And I fight to stand in a storm filled with acid rain. And I know what to do when I'm down. I come here. To my happy place. And I stare down at you, down at Earth, and I say "Cupid, no seas tan exagerada, boba *mira.*" This world is a never-ending lava lamp filled with Love. They'll be okay. You'll be okay."

And then I'd feel...limpia. Refreshed. Ready to keep fighting...

¿Entonces? Sáname pues. Por favor...

(A long pause.)

You're not some kind of never-ending pool of love, are you?

You know what I think of this view now?

(Slight pause. Then she spits viciously down onto Earth.)

CUPID. I see better views in IMAX pendejos!

(A beat.)

Fuck. It.

(She grabs her wings and makes sounds of pain as she pulls and pulls. With one last tremendous yank, she pulls her wings from her back with a cry of pain and surprise.)

(The wings fall apart, raining feathers down on Earth below.)

(She lays down on her rock, back bloody, trying to catch her breathe.)

(Darkness falls on her as she holds herself, trying to find comfort.)

Scene Two

*(A bedroom of an apartment in Hackensack, NJ. **ALEJANDRO** is sleeping in bed. **BENNY**, next to him, is not. His is sitting up wide awake. Outside the window of the bedroom, we see Cupid's feathers falling like snow. **BENNY** sees.)*

BENNY. Snow? Snow! Oh yay it's snowing...

Ain't it July?

*(He looks at **ALEJANDRO** sleeping.)*

Baby – are you awake?

(He keeps on sleeping and snoring.)

*(**BENNY** shoves him awake.)*

ALEJANDRO. FUCK!

BENNY. You awake?

ALEJANDRO. YES. You scared the shit outta me.

BENNY. Did you see that it's snowing?

ALEJANDRO. I was *asleep.*

BENNY. Oh. Right.

*(**ALEJANDRO** rolls over.)*

You're going back to sleep?

ALEJANDRO. I'm just exercising my eyelids. Gimme a few minutes to finish this set.

BENNY. I just had a bad dream though.

ALEJANDRO. OK.

*(He kisses **BENNY** a few times on the face.)*

ALEJANDRO. We good here?

(He rolls over again.)

BENNY. Alejo!

ALEJANDRO. Benny! I'm begging you. We were up late talking, and I need to be up early for work –

BENNY. I need to tell you about this dream, I think it's important.

ALEJANDRO. Lemme give you a handjob –

BENNY. What? No!

ALEJANDRO. It will relax you, come here papi –

BENNY. Alejandro stop! The world is ending.

ALEJANDRO. ...How?

BENNY. It's snowing, snowing in July. Literally look outside right now Alejo. Snow. July.

ALEJANDRO. ...Okay.

BENNY. And – and – politics are terrible, and the world is out to get us, people like me and you – to kill us and I just had a bad dream, a very bad dream. So I don't need you to give me a handjob, I don't need kisses, I need you to be a good boyfriend / and sit up and stop sleeping and //snoring and LISTEN TO ME.

ALEJANDRO. /Benny.

//OKKKKKKKKKKK.

(He sits up properly.)

Dale.

BENNY. Thank you.

So. In the dream.

I was hiding. Behind a corner of a wall, kinda like the one in the kitchen? And I'm holding a gun, a shotgun, and I'm holding it so tight that the veins on the back of my hand are making this angry little map –

And I started to feel this heat creepin' up on my leg. Almost like a small child was pressed up against it. And you and I are terrified –

ALEJANDRO. Hold up, hold up. I was there?

BENNY. Yeah – well I think you were. It felt like you were there, but I couldn't see you. It's like metaphorically you were there. Oh maybe you the gun?

ALEJANDRO. Why am I the gun?

BENNY. Because you're violent.

ALEJANDRO. No I'm not!

(Beat.)

Maybe a little but I'm not violent enough to be a gun, shit, a fuckin' shotgun at that –

BENNY. Can you let me finish please?

ALEJANDRO. I'm just trying to help you!

(Muttering.) You the gun.

BENNY. Violence is violence, is all I'm saying. Whether it's taking a gun out and shooting someone or it's being mean to someone you love in front of a group of friends...

(Pause.)

ALEJANDRO. I apologized Benny.

BENNY. It was just an example, I'm not saying it has specifically anything to do with you or tonight –

ALEJANDRO. I apologized –

BENNY. *And* I accepted, I'm just saying you're violent.

ALEJANDRO. I, Alejandro Diaz, am violent. My love, Benny Randle, is not. Are we done with the dream journaling now? Or is there something else you're trying to say?

(*A pause before* **BENNY** *goes to speak.*)

BENNY. ...Maybe the dream, the whole dream, it represents everything in our lives.

(**ALEJANDRO** *begins nodding off.*)

Our family. Our friends. Everything we share. So maybe you're the gun and *I'm* the bullet, and the child in the dream is –

(*He claps –* **ALEJANDRO** *wakes.*)

Stay. Awake. Please.

ALEJANDRO. I don't know...maybe the child in the dream...is ours?

BENNY. Oh don't say that. No no no. Why would you say that? To make me upset?

ALEJANDRO. You asked me to help you figure the dream out!

BENNY. I asked you to listen not input!

You know I don't want kids. No children. No pets, no plants. I want nothing tethering me to this world when I die. I want to float into the afterlife like a motherfucking balloon.

ALEJANDRO. And where does that leave me?

(*Another pause as* **BENNY** *goes to speak.*)

BENNY. You know what! I think I got it. I know what the child in the dream is. What it represents –

ALEJANDRO. Benny, por fa, just get to –

BENNY. Just this one last thing and I'll let you sleep.

The child. It's Love. Ours, I think. It's tiny, small, and afraid. And I'm doing my best to protect it, with everything I got, but no matter what I do, it's still in such danger...

(He trails off at the look on **ALEJANDRO**'s *face.)*

ALEJANDRO. ¿Cómo que? Did you just call our love a child?

BENNY. Um...

ALEJANDRO. Not only a child, but one that's scared and afraid?

BENNY. Well...Okay! Let's go sleepy time now. Night!

(He goes to bed. **ALEJANDRO** *gets up.)*

ALEJANDRO. Oh hell no – sleepy time over.

No. No Benny, no sleeping.

(He yanks the covers off the bed.)

BENNY. Alejandro, it was just a dream. I wasn't...

It was whatever okay? I don't know why you mad.

ALEJANDRO. Hm lemme see. The man who has been my partner for six years equates our love to that of a scared little child. Our love isn't a child. / A healthy relationship, the kind I want, between two grown ass men, should be – our love should be fucking ancient, okay? Old. Old as fuck. Older than the oldest thing in el puto mundo. Love should be a functioning // –

BENNY. / I wasn't saying it to upset you...

// Is it functioning?

(A silence.)

ALEJANDRO. Say what's on your mind.

BENNY. ...I am

ALEJANDRO. No you not. You been distant all day, we go out with friends tonight and you pick a fight –

BENNY. *You* picked a fight –

ALEJANDRO. *(Continued.)* And now you wake me up in the middle of the night to what? What Benny? Wax poetic about dreams and insult *my* relationship –

BENNY. It's our relationship, fifty/fifty, I can insult it if I want to –

ALEJANDRO. I know you Benny.

You get this anxious and ram-bly when you're dancing around an issue you don't want to deal with. So let's put away the tap shoes. Enough avoiding, evading. Say what you want to say.

(A pause.)

Benny. Open mouth. Move tongue. Say words.

(A long silence.)

(Their apartment dims as a warm gold light shines on the fire escape as **VALENTINE** *appears.)*

(He is dressed in golds and bright colors, a living portrait of a saint on a fresco, painted into the world by Gustav Klimt.)

(He stands for a moment, majestic, and we hear a celestial choir as he poses.)

VALENTINE. Shitty fuck. Did I miss it?

(He looks into the apartment, he checks a notebook he has.)

Benny and Alejandro – Yes! Just made it.

(He does a victory dance.)

Who the Saint? I'm the Saint. Who the Saint? I'm the Saint.

(Lights come back up on **BENNY** *and* **ALEJANDRO** *as* **VALENTINE** *watches.)*

ALEJANDRO. Say. *Words.* Benny.

BENNY. I've just been thinking lately…and I don't know if. We. Are…should keep on…doing us…or whatever.

(Silence.)

*(***VALENTINE*** cackles in the silence.)*

VALENTINE. Fucking Mary, Jesus and Joseph. That's a good one. Oh that's great – I gotta write that down.

(He scribbles in the notebook.)

*(***ALEJANDRO*** stares at* **BENNY***.)*

(After a beat, he goes to the window. He picks up a feather in the windowsill.)

ALEJANDRO. It wasn't snow.

BENNY. …What?

ALEJANDRO. It wasn't snow. They're feathers.

(As he holds a feather up to the light in the bedroom, **VALENTINE** *looks up from his notebook and sees the feather in* **ALEJANDRO***'s hand.)*

VALENTINE. …Cupid?

(He reaches down and looks at the feathers that have piled on the fire escape. He gathers them in his hands.)

VALENTINE. Oh no. Oh nonono. Fuck –

(He disappears in a gold light.)

(In the bedroom, **ALEJANDRO** *plays with the feather.)*

BENNY. I can't tell what you're thinking.

ALEJANDRO. Could you ever?

(He closes the window hard.)

I don't think I have a word for it. The feeling I'm feeling.

BENNY. Maybe it's a new one? Something new never felt before?

Maybe we can...name the new feeling –

ALEJANDRO. *(Abruptly.)* Can you go and stay with your tía?

BENNY. Well – yes but –

ALEJANDRO. Or I can go to a hotel.

BENNY. Alejandro it's the middle of the night

ALEJANDRO. Hotel or tía? Just answer hotel or tía Benny –

BENNY. Let's just take a second. Maybe we can, we can talk –

ALEJANDRO. Ay sí, ¿quieres hablar papi? Bueno pues ¿de que quieres hablar? ¿Hablar de nosotros? ¿Recuerdos de los ultimos seis años de ser novios? ¿Hablar de sueños? ¿de nieve? ¿de plumas? ¡¿Hablar de todas las peleas que hemos tenido en los últimos meses?! Or or OR, sabes qué, we can talk about the fact that the last time you kissed me was *JANUARY*.

(A beat.)

Any of those topics tickle your interest for conversation?

(Slight pause.)

I'm gonna go for a run. Please. *Please.*

Don't be here when I'm back.

(He goes.)

Scene Three

(Back in the heavens above Earth.)

*(**CUPID** is sitting down on her asteroid.)*

*(A flash of gold light – **VALENTINE** appears behind her.)*

(He takes in her torn back, bloody and wingless.)

(He quickly flips through his notebook and reads aloud.)

VALENTINE. "You, yourself, as much as anybody in the entire Universe, deserve your love and affection." Who / said that?

CUPID. / The Buddha.

(He flips to a new page.)

VALENTINE. "A Life without Love is sunless..." –

CUPID. Oscar Wilde. Your game is wack today pendejo.

VALENTINE. "Love is like a weed in a garden. It will grow and grow until you pluck it, but you must learn to let it grow."

Who said that smartass?

(A pause as she tries and fails.)

HA. How's it feel to lose so hard?

CUPID. Who said it?

VALENTINE. *(Gestures to himself.)* Who else?

CUPID. Love can't be a weed who want's a weedy fucking garden / choking out your flowers?

VALENTINE. / It's a metaphor!

CUPID. A *bad* one.

VALENTINE. *You're* a bad one.

CUPID. Valentine you really don't wanna annoy me right now –

       (**VALENTINE** *kisses her.*)

VALENTINE. Hello, Old Love.

CUPID. …Hello, Old Love.

VALENTINE. I think you dropped something.

       (*He shows her a feather.*)

       (**CUPID** *touches it lightly.*)

CUPID. Where did they land?

VALENTINE. Jersey.

CUPID. Guacala.

I was hoping for someplace pretty. Santa Marta, Rio, Madrid. A city from my heyday. A place that used to drip with amor…

VALENTINE. Don't knock Jersey my dear. Just cause they're fucking under boardwalks and turnpikes instead of the Eiffel Tower, doesn't make their celebrations of love any different.

CUPID. *(Snapping.)* Don't patronize me Valentine.

VALENTINE. I'm not –

CUPID. There isn't any love left in the world. Just heartbreak, pain, and death scattered everywhere like nasty, dirty, snow –

VALENTINE. Maybe you wouldn't think that, if you spent more time with the people down there instead of glaring at them from on high –

CUPID. I spent enough. More than enough. Cupid has ripped off her wings, she's quitting the job, leaving with her middle finger up, screaming "Cómeme el CULO" to everyone who bothers to listen.

> *(She grabs the feather from him and throws it away from her.)*

> *(Silence as* **CUPID** *puts her back to him and hugs her knees.)*

> *(***VALENTINE*** *breathes in deeply, then blows out.)*

> *(The stars around them flare brighter in response.)*

VALENTINE. You sit in the dark long enough, everything is gonna look that way.

Umbria, Italy...

CUPID. Valentine...

> *(He moves closer.)*

VALENTINE. In the third century...

CUPID. I'll push you off this fucking rock –

VALENTINE. There, in that time and place, the God of Love found a letter written by a dead man. The man had been a priest and healer who performed secret marriage ceremonies. Something illegal, in that time and place.

He admitted freely to the crimes when arrested. Instead of a fair trial, he demanded, annoyed and harassed the guards for pen and paper to write a letter. A love letter. To his jailer's daughter.

With a signature at the bottom, "From Your Valentine"...

After reading the letter, Cupid flew to the filthy pit where they had thrown the man's body. He had been beaten, whipped, and beheaded...Cupid washed the body clean...kissed the bruised throat...and watched as the body melted away like gold Florida water and left in its place...the man, whole. Saintly.

When the man asked Cupid why, she said...?

(*A pause. She doesn't respond.*)

"...because I liked your letter."

(*Slight pause.*)

CUPID. I hate hearing about the past Valentine. And I don't care even a little about the future. But thank you for that beautiful letter.

(*She gets up away from him.*)

VALENTINE. So you're quitting. Just like that?

Can Gods even quit?

CUPID. Who cares? I do / whatever the fuck I want.

VALENTINE. / Whatever you want yea yea yeah. So you're just gonna pass the centuries sitting here doing what? Picking at your ass and whittling?

CUPID. Who says I'm staying here?

(*She snaps.*)

(*The blackness of space around them ripples, churns.*)

(*And a door appears, outlined in a strange light.*)

VALENTINE. ...What the hell is that?

CUPID. A door.

VALENTINE. You sure I thought it was a new type of elephant – OF COURSE IT'S A DOOR.

...You're gonna leave?

Where does that even go?

CUPID. Away. That's all I care about away away away –

VALENTINE. You can't just give up –

CUPID. I've already given up!

I upgraded arrows to bullets I've shot people by the millions –

I can't get Love to stick. It just withers and dies the minute I look away...

VALENTINE. What the hell happened to you?

CUPID. Nada.

VALENTINE. We've been through terrible times before and you were always the first one back on her feet.

Something must have happened.

> *(Silence.)*

I'll find out eventually Cupid.

CUPID. You're not gonna find out shit.

VALENTINE. I know you better than anyone. We're lovers without limits, best friends, co-workers even –

> *(He stops as* **CUPID** *snorts.)*

...what was that?

CUPID. Nothing a sneeze keep going.

VALENTINE. We are coworkers.

CUPID. Whatever you say mi rey.

VALENTINE. I am the Patron Saint of Love.

CUPID. And that is adorable on you.

VALENTINE. It's an important job –

CUPID. You stand outside windows watching relationships *end*, then scribble shit in your little notebook. You're the Patron Saint of Voyeurs and Idiotic Perverts!

VALENTINE. ...How DARE you...

You've NEVER understood my work. The flower cannot bloom in the Spring without death in the winter –

CUPID. Ay por favor –

VALENTINE. *(Continued.)* Relationships are cyclical, and we can learn a lot about love when –

CUPID. Oh fuck you, you hipster wannabee intellectual pendejo.

VALENTINE. Fuck you – you...dumb...lady

CUPID. I'm leaving.

VALENTINE. It's that easy then? To leave me.

> *(Silence.)*

> *(She picks up her shotgun and goes to the door.)*

I won't let you.

> *(She points the gun at him for a moment.)*

CUPID. Is that really the note you want us to end on?

> *(A tense pause.)*

> *(She points the gun away.)*

You could come.

VALENTINE. I'm not running away from the problems of the world.

CUPID. You're better than me.

VALENTINE. No one's better than you.

> *(Slight pause.)*

CUPID. All the fight I had in the past…it's transformed into something small inside me. A little animal curled up in a ball, afraid of the light.

And I don't want to be that person to the world. To *you*.

So I need to go. OK?

> *(She puts her hand on the door.)*

VALENTINE. Hug me goodbye? Cupid please. Give me that at least?

> *(Long pause.)*
>
> *(She goes back to him and he swoops her into a big embrace.)*

CUPID. You're gonna kill me.

VALENTINE. Good than you can't leave.

CUPID. *(Laughs.)* Careful Valentine. I still have my shotgun.

VALENTINE. That's true.

> *(Holding her he steps close to the edge.)*

But you know what you don't have any more Cupid?

CUPID. *(Confused.)* What?

VALENTINE. Wings.

> *(He kicks them off the asteroid.)*

CUPID. OH YOU FUCKING HIJO DE LA GRAN PUTA!

(We see them fall to Earth as **THE POET** *speaks.)*

THE POET. Limbs entangled, Valentine holding her with all he's got, they stream towards Earth below like a comet in a golden light.

Scene Four

(Back in the apartment.)

(ALEJANDRO *is working out so hard – it looks unhealthy.)*

ALEJANDRO. I am single now.

I am hot. I don't need Benny. I don't need nobody cause this ass is Fyne with a y. I am hot, hot like sancocho on a summer's night WOOOO.

(He works out harder.)

Alexa. Open Grindr.

(We hear **ALEXA**. **ALEXA** *and the* **SCRUFF VOICES** *can be voiced by* **THE POET**.*)*

ALEXA. You have zero messages on Grindr.

ALEJANDRO. Alexa open Tinder.

You have zero matches on Tinder.

(He runs faster.)

Alexa open Scruff.

ALEXA. You have three messages on Scruff.

ALEJANDRO. Fuck Yeah I do Mamita! Read messages.

ALEXA. Reading messages.

SCRUFF USER #1. Omg are you uncut –

ALEJANDRO. Delete. Next.

SCRUFF USER #2. Wanna fuck this pussy?

ALEJANDRO. Maybe. Actually, no. In the mood for something else, keep reading.

(He works harder, lungs bursting, sweat pouring.)

SCRUFF USER #3. I like your smile.

*(**ALEJANDRO** is surprised by the sweetness. So surprised, he makes a misstep then slams hard.)*

ALEJANDRO. My. Fucking Rib…

ALEXA. Playing "My Rib!" By Nick Cannon!

ALEJANDRO. No – Alexa stop – don't.

(He gets up and he checks his phone. The guy is cute.)

Alexa dictate message.

"Hey, yours too. It's…wow."

Send.

*(A pause. He picks up a photo of him and **BENNY** nearby.)*

(He looks at it. Takes it out. Almost rips it in half. Stops.)

Alexa, new message, same user.

"Hey. Before you respond. Let me say something.

You're cute. You think I'm cute. Great – we passed that first round. Now we can move on to the next and talk about museums, things we like – our favorite music, yadda yadda. We can plan a date and try to get to know each other. And as we do know each other, we'll start to hurt each other. It will start with little things, tiny burns here and there, until they grow into full out attacks. Either way, in the long run…we'll just be hurt.

So let's not bother with the whole thing.

ALEJANDRO. I can be ready in thirty minutes. You can come over and I can fuck you silly. I won't even tell you my name. And when the cum is out and the breath is back in our lungs, we can hold each other and act like we've got someone who cares. All for less than half an hour.

We'll get the fix we need to make it to the next day.

Safer this way."

Send.

(He puts the photo aside, then starts working out again.)

*(**ALEXA** beeps.)*

ALEXA. You have one new / message –

ALEJANDRO. / Read.

SCRUFF USER #3. "...Address?"

*(**ALEJANDRO** runs with all he's got.)*

Scene Five

(A dentist's office in Hackensack.)

*(**BENNY** is lying in a dentist's chair.)*

*(**BETTI**, a dental hygienist, is checking something off a form.)*

*(Nearby a **REPORTER** is heard on a radio.)*

REPORTER. Meteorologists around the globe are reporting a new comet moving through the upper stratospheres of Earth. Not made of any type of rock, it is believed to be comprised of pure light, moving towards Earth at a frightening speed. Though scientists report we have nothing to fear in terms of negative effects, radio systems around the globe continue to pick up interference from said comet. Broadcasts are continuously interrupted by loud static, and what some swear is *language*. Reports are flying in by the hundreds as citizens around the Globe attest to hearing what sounds like two people arguing in extremely vulgar Spanish and English.

One Million Moms has begun a campaign to temporarily –

*(**BENNY** leans over and turns off the radio.)*

BENNY. Is that okay if I...?

BETTI. Oh Sure! Whatever you want. I'm a bit of a news junkie so...

BENNY. I was afraid that would break some rule, touching without permission...

BETTI. There are no rules here. Except maybe no biting.

BENNY. Ha.

BETTI. Ha.

(Awkward silence.)

BENNY. The news reminds me of my boyfriend.

BETTI. That's nice!

BENNY. Sorry, I mean ex-boyfriend.

BETTI. Oh! Well, that's...sorry.

BENNY. No no! It's totally okay. I broke up with him.

BETTI. Oh! Well...men are dogs. Or so I'm told...

BENNY. No he's a good guy, we like him. You know how these things happen sometimes...

(Slight pause.)

BETTI. ...I'm sorry, I don't know what the appropriate reaction here should be.

(Silence. She goes back to her prep work.)

BENNY. It's been two months since the break up and I've been doing yoga – namaste – and I've gotten really spiritual about Alejandro, my ex. Wishing the best I could wish for him in his future...without me.

I'm also going to the gym every other week, I've gotten a check up with my doctor, got an eye exam (twenty/twenty vision), went to the ear nose and throat doctor (my sinuses – glitter and gold). And now I'm here with you. I'm on this chapter of new slates and new beginnings.

BETTI. That's great. I feel like most people let everything go when they're going through heartbreak –

BENNY. I'm not going through heartbreak.

BETTI. Oh, I just meant –

BENNY. I broke up with him I'm fine.

BETTI.   Right. Well, I was just gonna say if you open /
your...

BENNY.   / My mind is open I am open like...

(He makes a gesture and sound of "openness".)

What's your name again?

BETTI.   ...Betti...

BENNY.   I'm open Betti.

Alejandro was slash is my first love. And I care about
him deeply, but "openness" ain't the problem here. It's
just...

Have you ever woken up one day and realized a pair of
pants you loved, fit you weird?

That's what happened to me... I just woke up one day
and realized that this shit didn't fit anymore.

The night we broke up I looked over at Alejandro
while he was sleeping and I could feel this pressure.
PRESSURE Betti, lemme tell you. In that moment, it
felt like if I turned around, I would see everyone in the
world behind me. Everyone I knew – mouths foaming,
pushing and shoving me into this, this, this, fucking
OCEAN of commitment.

And I'm on the brink of the water, digging in with my
heels for my life – I mean my motherfuckin' life – cause
fuck yeah I'm terrified Betti! I'm not ready to swim in
that ocean yet! I've never practiced in other waters,
with other people, I haven't even practiced in a kiddie
pool. Like I should practice in a little itty bitty pool
with those water wingies first – cause yes I am a grown
man, I do my own taxes now, really I do – but what am
I in the scheme of the world?

An infant. A child...

BENNY. I'm not ready to dive into this ocean now, maybe I never will be...

(*Pause.*)

(**BETTI** *goes to speak, cut off by the following;*)

So I feel all this pressure while I look at Alejandro sleeping next to me –

And – and – I'm sorry what were we talking about?

BETTI. I had said open –

BENNY. OPEN, that's right. I was and I am open. Betti. Betti, right?

BETTI. It's Betti.

(*A long silence.*)

What I was going to say is that if you lie back and open your mouth...I can get your cleaning going...

BENNY. Oh. Okay.

(*He leans back and* **BETTI** *gets to work.*)

BETTI. That was really impressive. The things you said.

I'll be quite honest that I didn't understand...all of it? But it sounded really...thought out.

Working in the dental field you see your fair share of people who can really stitch together a sentence but that was...

My own experience with love is...I guess if love for you, was this ocean –

I've never seen its waters.

(*She cleans.*)

You should floss more.

(Keeps cleaning.)

I've always been rather clinical. I think that's why I ended up here, doing this. It's straight forward work for the right person. And that's me – straightforward. Love, relationships, sex, always seemed to be for people that were more...I don't know. Elaborate. Grand. People that had bigger, epic lives filled with fireworks and color. Less straightforward.

*(**BENNY** speaks a garbled mess of something as she cleans.)*

Oh thanks that's sweet, but I don't mind it. For a while I thought I was asexual, but I went to a meeting? For asexuals? And everyone there seemed really...like they weren't necessarily looking for anyone because inside, they already had that answered. And that's not me, for sure. I've always been looking. For what...or who I can't say.

(She continues cleaning.)

It might have something to do with my parents.

My mom was an American Citizen, and my Dad wasn't, so they originally just got together without intending any romance. They just wanted the papers so my father could live here. It was a business transaction. They told me that they happened to be lonely one night and... voilà. Me.

I'm going to have to go a bit deeper now.

(She goes deeper into his mouth.)

With everything happening in the world right now – snow in July, comets heading towards Earth – I don't know if I've been in just a pensive kind of place, but I've been thinking about my parents' situation a lot. And the circumstances in which they had me?

BETTI. I think maybe that's why I never feel in love. Because I was made in...loneliness rather than love? I'm more Loneliness's daughter than I am of anyone else.

Probably accounts for why I never...

Anyways.

> *(She finishes cleaning. Removes her hands from* **BENNY***'s mouth.)*

OK Benny! You're all set. Dr. Geffe will come in and –

> *(***BENNY*** is weeping in the chair.)*

Oh! Oh no – did I hurt you?

BENNY. YES YOU FUCKING HURT ME. Did you hear what you just said? Loneliness's Daughter? That's the saddest shit I've ever fuckin heard...

> *(***BETTI*** swivels in her chair, unsure. She grabs something from the counter nearby.)*

BETTI. Would you like a free toothbrush?!

BENNY. Y – yes.

> *(He takes it.)*

BETTI. I'm so sorry. I shouldn't have said those things. You were just so open with me and I just felt that deserved openness in kind and...

> *(She cries.)*

BENNY. Why are you crying?

BETTI. I don't know.

> *(They cry together for a quick beat.)*
>
> *(Then they laugh.)*

(A spark passes between them.)

BENNY. I'm sorry –

BETTI. Don't apologize –

BENNY. I'm walking around like a raw nerve...

BETTI. Why don't you call him? Alejandro?

BENNY. He won't talk to me, since the night of the break up...

BETTI. Why did you break up with him?

> *(Quick pause.)*

That's none of my business / I'm sorry.

BENNY. / Would you have dinner with me?

BETTI. ...What?

BENNY. Tonight?

> *(Silence. Slowly,* **BENNY** *puts his hand on* **BETTI***'s.)*

We can be lonely together?

BETTI. ...Okay.

Scene Six

(A park, daytime, in Hackensack a few days later.)

(The park has begun to shimmer golden. It goes brighter and brighter until – a monstrous crash is heard.)

(Silence.)

(Two holes are in the ground at the park.)

(From one – we see an arm emerge. Dragging himself out is **VALENTINE***.)*

VALENTINE. My. Fucking. BACK...

(He places his hands on lower back as he stretches.)

Actually...I think the fall was good – my back feels great.

(He takes in the park around him.)

AND we landed in a park. Beautiful sun, green glowing grass –

(He hums a little jazzy tune to himself as he takes in the park*. Then he looks at the other hole apprehensively.)

So.

How are / you –

---

*A license to produce *I Wanna Fuck Like Romeo and Juliet* does not include a performance license for any third-party or copyrighted music. Licensees should create an original composition or use music in the public domain. For further information, please see the Music and Third-Party Materials Use Note on page iii.

(/ A scream of pure rage is heard.)

(VALENTINE *quickly sits on the hole covering it up.)*

(Muffled screams are heard through the following;)

OK! I'm sensing you might be a little mad.

And if you look at it a certain way, you have a right to be. I fucked up your exit strategy, brought you back to the Earth you have forsaken. Forsooken? What's the word again babe is it forsaken or –

*(More screams and **VALENTINE** is nearly thrown off.)*

But if you look at this whole situation Cupid – this is mostly your fault! You are trying to shirk your responsibilities, responsibilities that you swore to the Heavens that you would spend your immortal life doing. Don't let these dangerous good looks fool you, Old Love, I am first and foremost a man of the cloth, and I believe vows to be sacro...sacril...very FUCKING SPECIAL.

You might hate me right now Cupid but I am doing this FOR YOU.

(Silence. The screams have stopped.)

(He waits tense for a beat, then relaxes.)

Okey Dokey Lemon Soakey.

I'm going to let you out now. And then we're gonna talk this out like two civilized deities with a long history together that –

(CUPID *shoots* **VALENTINE** *– in his ass.)*

FUCK the POPE AHHHH.

(He jumps away from the hole, screaming in pain.)

*(**CUPID** claws her way out of the hole, a vengeance on two legs.)*

CUPID. HIJO DE LA GRAN PUTA –

VALENTINE. *(Through pain.)* OK, definitely mad –

CUPID. DOBLE, TRIPLE, HIJUEPUTA! GONORREA, CULICAGADO –

VALENTINE. Who shoots first before cursing someone out?!

(She shoots him in the knee.)

Holy TRINITY!

CUPID. Take me back. RIGHT. NOW.

VALENTINE. Or WHAT.

CUPID. I FUCKING shoot you.

VALENTINE. YOU'VE BEEN SHOOTING ME.

Keep shooting me, I'm a saintly fucking immortal and I'm not taking you back to SHIT. What the fuck are you gonna do about it?

CUPID. I'll keep shooting you until I run out of bullets. And if you don't remember, La Loca? Never runs out of bullets.

*(**VALENTINE** stumbles to his feet. Looks around for a weapon. Out of options – He adapts a lame karate pose. **CUPID** cocks the gun.)*

(A brief tense pause.)

VALENTINE. Let me just say one thing first.

CUPID. WHAT?

> *(He points behind her.)*

VALENTINE. What's that?

CUPID. ...I'm not looking behind me Valentine.

VALENTINE. ...That's not what I'm doing.

CUPID. Yes it is.

VALENTINE. How do you know if you haven't looked?

CUPID. Because you're a fucking idiot that's how I know.

VALENTINE. Just look. Just look / just look, just look, JUST LOOK.

CUPID. / No. No. No NO FINE!

> *(She looks and then he's speeding away in a gold flash.)*
>
> *(With a scream of frustration* **CUPID** *jumps to fly...)*
>
> *(And falls to the floor pathetically...)*
>
> *(A few beats she fumes.)*
>
> *(She turns touching her back and hisses in pain.)*
>
> *(She gets to her feet and grabs her gun to follow when –.)*
>
> *(We hear a voice from off.)*

BETTI. GUN! OH MY GOD GUN GUN GUN

> *(***CUPID*** jumps in surprise.)*

CUPID. La PUTA madre.

(**BETTI** *continues to scream.*)

(**CUPID** *drops the gun and puts her hands up.*)

CUPID. Tranquila! Tranquila! CALM DOWN! IT'S A – A COSTUME OKAY? The gun isn't real.

(*The screaming stops.*)

BETTI. (*Quietly.*) ...What?

CUPID. It's a costume, okay? I'm on my way to a costume party.

(*A brief pause.*)

BETTI. Oh.

(**BETTI** *walks in. She's wearing a formal nightgown.*)

I don't think I ever screamed like that in my life, sorry.

CUPID. Can I grab my gun or will you start screaming again?

BETTI. I'm done.

(*She grabs it.*)

You might want to be careful walking with that though. There are so many shootings and –

CUPID. I don't need a reminder of how awful the world is, Okay? I'm aware...

(**CUPID** *looks at* **BETTI** *in surprise.*)

You see me.

BETTI. ...Yes?

CUPID. ...How?

BETTI. Because you're...standing...in front of me...

CUPID. It's just normally people don't –

BETTI. *(Re: her back.)* Oh no you're bleeding!

CUPID. Oh – it's just a scratch.

BETTI. That doesn't look like just a scratch –

CUPID. *Really.* I'm fine.

BETTI. Alright...

I'm Betti?

CUPID. I'm Cu...

> *(Slight pause.)*

Cuepeeda.

BETTI. Cuepeeda?

CUPID. Hm hmmm. Cupeda it's Greek.

BETTI. ...Nice to meet you?

CUPID. Same...

Nice dress.

BETTI. Oh Thank you! I'm going on a date. Or I guess it's more like a...half-date?

I'm meeting someone for coffee on the other side of the park.

CUPID. Ah...new Love.

BETTI. Oh god, oh no no. He's sweet but mostly gay? And I think I might be mostly gay? I'm still figuring it out...

CUPID. Then why are you –

BETTI. Practice. And before you think I'm a monster, he's going through a breakup and I think he might be using me to avoid loneliness. So me using him, while he's using me, is kind of a mutually beneficial, equally monster-y sort of thing to do.

BETTI. I'm treating it all like "dating school". I'm taking every outing with Benny as a different lesson. Today, I'm focusing on wearing formal wear and laughing. Last time I went out with Benny I laughed like this –

> *(She laughs like she's on a date.)*

But today –

> *(She laughs another way.)*

Growth!...

This is all too much isn't it?

I heard how it all sounded when I said it out loud...

I should stop seeing him shouldn't I?

CUPID. Lo siento nena, but I'm currently transitioning *out* of a profession where I give people advice on love.

BETTI. Therapist?

CUPID. More like...a relationship coach.

BETTI. Oh my – wow – This is perfect.

Can I ask some questions? Professionally I mean.

CUPID. I need to get going –

BETTI. I just want to know about kissing! Not that I haven't kissed before. I went to book camp...

I just mean, it's always felt so...*plain*. A day old bagel.

Is there something I should focus on? Maybe a certain way to shape my mouth –

CUPID. I really need –

BETTI. But if you could answer this one –

CUPID. *(Snaps.)* You want advice?! There is no good advice, because it's all terrible. I think it's terrible, I think you're terrible, I think ALL OF THIS –

(She gestures to the world around them –.)

Is *terrible*.

BETTI. ...This park?

CUPID. The whole world. Everyone in this whole world is drenched in poison and hate.

(Slight pause.)

BETTI. That's so...WOW

Sad.

Oh god I think even my *bones* are sad after hearing that.

CUPID. Welcome to how I feel all the time.

*(A beat as **CUPID** wrestles with the silence.)*

BETTI. You must have really loved it.

CUPID. What?

BETTI. The world. I don't think you can feel that sad about something without having loved it first.

*(A beat as **CUPID** and **BETTI** look at each other.)*

(A spark passes between them.)

We haven't met before right?

CUPID. I don't think so...

BETTI. I think we might have...you just look...familiar. I hope you don't mind me saying this but you look...

(A quick beat.)

Kind of like a ring I lost when I was eight, then I found again when I was fifteen? Not losing the ring or finding it again.

BETTI. You look like the space in between.

Like Hope?

I'm not good at explaining things...

But you look like Hope.

(*A silence as* **CUPID** *really takes her in.*)

CUPID. ...You want advice?

BETTI. Yes of course! Should I maybe write this down –

CUPID. One – do you like what you're wearing? This dress?

BETTI. We're starting right in, okay great!

Oh you know...

It's pretty uh...horrible.

CUPID. Burn it. Wear what you feel good in. You'd look great in a suit.

BETTI. A suit! Okay...

CUPID. Two – that laugh you did earlier? La que estaba practicando con "Benny"?

BETTI. The laugh? Oh the laugh! This one?

(*She laughs like before.*)

CUPID. Yeah that one.

En el nombre de todo lo sagrado...Never, ever, laugh that way again. You look so batshit loca, pero tan loca I can't even do it justice describing it...

BETTI. (*Overwhelmed.*) Oh, wow, well – Thank you for the / advice –

CUPID. / I'm not done.

BETTI. Yes Ma'am...

CUPID. Final thing – kissing should *never* feel…like an old bagel.

Kissing, is a sacred thing.

When someone kisses you, and it's a good kiss (which is rare), it should feel –

Like the nerves in your mouth are starting to sing…

> *(She gets closer to* **BETTI***.)*

> *(The lights go red around them.)*

> *(***BETTI*** is captivated by her words.)*

Y cantan en un coro en la iglesia de tu cuerpo.

BETTI. *(Dazed.)* How am I…I'm understanding you…I've never really understood Spanish –

CUPID. Cállate Betti.

BETTI. Si señora.

CUPID. Y mientras sus labios tocan los tuyos, la voz del coro crece y crece

BETTI. …Like a kiss in crescendo?

CUPID. Aja.

> *(She's very close to* **BETTI***'s lips right now.)*

¿Puedo?

BETTI. *(Confused, still dazed.)* …Wha?

…Can you what?

> *(Pause.)*

OH! *(Quietly.)* Holy shit…Um.

> *(She looks around.)*

I would like that very much.

(A beat.)

(Then **CUPID** *kisses* **BETTI**. *Deeply.)*

(The lights of **THE POET** *explode across their bodies in a splash of light.)*

(We hear the voice of **THE POET** *as* **CUPID** *continues to kiss* **BETTI** *deeply.)*

THE POET. Cupid, rarely kisses people anymore.

But the people she's kissed...

Sor Juana. Lorca.

Kahlo. Basquiat. De Saint Phalle.

Baldwin. Policarpa.

Sappho. Rumi...

Cupid doesn't kiss you with just her lips.

When she kisses you, she crawls into a corner of your soul.

And...well...

Cupid *penetrates* your soul with a kiss.

> *(We see* **BETTI** *go a bit limp in* **CUPID**'s *arms.)*
>
> *(***CUPID** *eventually stops.)*
>
> *(The lights of* **THE POET** *fade, and the world returns to normal.* **BETTI** *opens her eyes and the two stare for a quick beat.)*
>
> *(They separate quickly.)*

CUPID. So, yeah, that's what a kiss / should be.

BETTI. / That was a really useful example, thank you so much.

CUPID. So I'm just...I'm gonna go and find my friend.

Suerte y pulso Betti.

> *(Pause.)*

You're...lovely.

> *(**CUPID** leaves quickly.)*

> *(A beat as **BETTI** sways.)*

> *(Then suddenly.)*

BETTI. BYE!

...

Bye I mean! In a normal tone!

Bye Cue...Pee..

> *(She touches her lips.)*

THE POET. Oh – oh – Betti!

Her first kiss was CUPID?!

That's...

Girl that's a lot...

> *(Slight beat.)*

In the part of Betti's soul that Cupid penetrated...

There is an effect...

A Rippling – a churning – a foaming – a *birthing*

Changing everything that is – or was – Betti.

> *(Finger snaps are overhead, multiple ones,
> overlapping until **BETTI** suddenly stands
> rock straight and speaks in a frenzy.)*

BETTI. I don't think Betti has ever had an inner voice, what Betti has instead is an inner *script*. I say Betti in the third person, because that's how my relationship with Betti has always been – *me* watching *Betti*, watching her follow her inner script. Never *living* because you don't need to live when you have a tidy little script that you follow from one moment to the next, days don't feel like days when you follow the script, it's just repeated moments and beats and that repetition, that is a tidy tight hug. and yes dear god sometimes that hug can be an *all consuming suffocation* but here we are thirty plus years and Betti has never ever deviated from the inner script that *SHE WROTE*. With the help of the world around her, and the Gods and fates and her parents and their non-love all helped Betti write her inner script but SHE WROTE IT- and things like anger and disappointment and boredom and loneliness are held at bay far away from Betti's – well of course you can't use the word *life* to describe what Betti has – but all those feelings of pain are kept far away from her scripted scripted *scripted* EXISTENCE and THEN she met Benny and decided to deviate just slightly because what's the harm in experiencing all those FEELINGS that the Script usually protects her from, and yes say yes to having dinner with Benny because for the first time in your life someone has seen more than just Betti's TIDY FUCKING SCRIPT! He's seen he's seen Benny saw and liked the flash of ME. Me me, the REAL ME, the one who just WATCHES Betti NOT LIVING, and –

This lady just gave me a real kiss, a kiss that –

> *(Then she touches her chest, like it's hard to breathe.)*

Can kisses affect your *lungs?!!!* Why do I feel like – like – like...

Why do I still feel her lips?!?! Am I having a STROKE?! Are phantom kisses a stroke symptom?! No one teaches you strokes in dental hygienist school –

Her lips are touching every particle –

Are gently pressing against every single cell of the Thirty-Seven Point Two Trillion that make up B – E – T – T – I the REAL BETTI, THE REAL ME

And every cell in response to the pressing of her lips is is is is IS

> *(She gasps and breathes like she's falling from the sky.)*

Every Cell inside me –

Is responding to her lips by –

Leaning back, into the hips and curves and gentle pushing of her lips, and everything IN ME THE REAL BETTI. THE ONE THAT WATCHES BUT NO LONGER IS HAPPY WATCHING! NOW AFTER THAT KISS EVERYTHING IS –

> *(Slight pause.)*

> *(She trills her mouth, makes insane sounds.* **BETTI** *comes close to losing her mind, before suddenly throwing her hands open in unbridled ecstasy as she's covered by the lights of* **THE POET**.*)*

> *(Screaming along to the voice of* **THE POET** *–.)*

BETTI.	THE POET.
OPENINGGGGGG!!!!!!!!	Bendito sea. Bendito Sea. Bendito Sea...

> (**BETTI** *looks around, dazed and a glow...*)

> *(She suddenly jerks forward like something pricked her back.)*

BETTI. OW! Mosquitos!

> *(She looks behind her.)*

> *(And plucks a small feather from her back and stares at it in wonder and confusion.)*

> (**BENNY** *walks on holding two coffees.)*

BENNY. Hey Betti!

> (**BETTI** *quickly hides the feather.)*

I got here a little early. Wow that's a...*(Lying through their teeth.)* Fierce dress girl!

> *(She doesn't respond.)*

Are you alright? You look like you saw a ghost.

BETTI. Oh no, not quite. I think I just saw more Life than anyone has ever seen before.

> *(She gasps in sudden shock and* **BENNY** *jumps in surprise.)*

DID YOU GET ME COFFEE?! Is this what boyfriends do?! Then yes please sign me up for another six weeks of relationship winter Benny!!!!!

BENNY. Uh well, I got myself a latte and...something you should know about me. I am VERY good at guessing people's coffee or tea of choice. It's like my version of reading tarot. And even though we've only had two dates between the teeth cleaning and the dinner (my teeth are still so shiny thank you again), I think I can safely say that YOU, Betti, are a Green Tea type of gal –

BETTI. Nope! Hate green tea! Tastes like dirty leaves.

BENNY. Oh...

BETTI. NO disappointment Benny! My entire existence was just reorganized. Maybe I do like Green Tea now!

(She grabs the tea from **BENNY**.*)*

BENNY. Oh careful it's –

(She downs the entire drink, unaffected by the heat, splashing herself like a maniac while **BENNY** *stares in shock.)*

...hot...

*(***BETTI*** then throws the empty tea behind her then screams.)*

BETTI. OH GOD DON'T LET THE NEW BETTI LITTER BENNY!

(She runs and grabs the cup she just threw.)

BENNY. You seem...uniquely...unique...today...

BETTI. It's a unique kind of day! A day of nothing but firsts. Do you like this dress? I don't! LOATHE it. Let's burn it! I've never burned a dress in a park before. We'll burn the dress, then find me a suit, then we can go lie naked and KISS by a river. THAT can be our newest date. That's something people do, right? When they're head over heels in love?!?!

BENNY. Love?! Oh Betti I don't know if I'm quite ready to throw that word around –

BETTI. Not in love with you, conceited! What am I, a maniac?!

(She laughs like a maniac.)

I'm in love with ME.

(She grabs **BENNY** *and gives him a passionate kiss.)*

*(It's not the same type of fireworks as her kiss with **CUPID** but it does knock the wind out of **BENNY**.)*

BENNY. Wow, that was...

BETTI. Not the best kiss – we don't have the right chemistry. Not to brag or anything but I'm now an absolute expert on the subject.

*(She grabs his hand to pull **BENNY** off.)*

Screw the practice date. I don't want to practice or just WATCH anything ever again. I only want to do. Do Do Dododo.

Let's find a river. I LOVE rivers. Rivers are very misunderstood things.

*(**BENNY** stops her.)*

BENNY. Betti, wait.

*(She stops. **BENNY** takes her hands.)*

You seem...

Like...a volcano that's in the middle of eruption.

All this monumental chaos you're suddenly brimming with is...

Honestly hot. But...

Are you the same Betti I met the other day?

BETTI. Benny – I'm the farthest from her I've ever been. Isn't that delicious?!

(She drags him off.)

Scene Eight

*(We see **BENNY** on the street. He's wearing scrubs.)*

*(He's staring up at the window of the apartment. We see **ALEJANDRO** sleeping above him like Juliet on the balcony or some shit.)*

*(While **BENNY** stares **VALENTINE** skids on, breathing hard and haggard. He then yelps in fear, then immediately calms when he see's it's **BENNY**.)*

VALENTINE. *(Yelps.)* Fuck the shitty Pope's BALLS, it's you. Benny.

(He looks around scared.)

I shot to Lodi, Passaic. She's chasing me all over New Jersey. Keeps popping out at me from the dark like a Chupa – Fucking – Cabra. You'd think she'd be *slower* without those stupid fucking wings. Oh Valentine you asshole don't say that, you love those beautiful fucking wings and you're stressed, this is stressful, isn't this STRESSFUL Benny!!!

What are we gonna do, what are we gonna do? This has always been my problem Benny, I don't like planning, sitting on the outside of something and waiting and talking and waiting and talking about it makes me want to chop off my own fucking head off again. I live my immortal life like the Saintly Fucking Kool-Aid Man, barreling through walls like OH YEAH instead of *thinking* about the fact that I didn't have a step two. I didn't even really have step one! My soul just short circuited when she moved to go through that door and now...

VALENTINE. I mean who are we without Cupid, Benny?! What's gonna happen to all of us with her gone?! Are Babies gonna start saying FUCK YOU instead of MAMA as their first words?! Flowers are never gonna bloom in the same way. Chocolate will blink out of existence, trust will be leaner, without any real meat to it I MEAN REALLY BENNY HELP ME OUT HERE, what's gonna HAPPEN to us?!

> *(Pause.)*

What's gonna happen to me?

> *(A beat.)*

Who am I, without her nearby?

> *(**VALENTINE** crumples and turns to **BENNY** with his hands out.)*

Can I have a hug?!

> *(He hugs **BENNY** and cries for a few loud beats.)*

You can't see or feel me – but this is still nice. I needed this. And you smell good. You smell like...

> *(He smells **BENNY**. Then he's confused.)*

Why do you smell like a dental hygienist?

> *(A beat as he wipes his face on **BENNY** shoulder and then really looks around for the first time.)*

And why are we out here in...

> *(He sees **ALEJANDRO** through the window.)*

Oh my God. Oh you beautiful idiot. This is so delicious, it must be fattening.

No wonder you keep pulling me across all the known Universe?! You're a romantic idiot under there, huh Benny? What do you think's gonna happen here? That Alejandro is gonna just happen to walk by the window in the middle of the night, in his sexiest lingerie, framed by a candle's warm cozy glow? And he's gonna look outside wishing, just wishing, Benny was there and BEHOLD there's Benny! Standing in the street like a totally normal person not an unhinged maniac...

Oh...

Benny...

...*Girl*...

> *(A longer pause.)*

Who am I to judge though? You got the right Saint with the right amount of limited time.

> (**BENNY** *shakes his head like girl you're an idiot and moves to go.*)

No no, come on, first instincts are good instincts.

> (**VALENTINE** *snaps and* **BENNY** *is bathed in a gold light.*)

Don't get scared now. Stay...

Listen to the voice in your ear that sounds like me.

Listen to the voice reminding you...

Remember with your senses.

Smell – the secret spice Alejandro loves putting in his cooking.

BENNY. *(To himself.)* Nutmeg...

VALENTINE. Feel – the curve of his lower back against your arm...

BENNY. Sweaty...

VALENTINE. Taste the scar under his left nipple –

BENNY. Salt and honey ridges...

VALENTINE. Hear the way he laughs

BENNY. *(Laughs remembering his laugh.)*

VALENTINE. Remember how he would make a bath for you whenever you were stressed.

When he punched that guy who called you a faggot at a bar.

Or how you much you loved the way he passionately hates kale.

When you would listen as he belted Celia Cruz in the shower.

How he always remembered your Mom's favorite flower is a purple orchid.

Remember when he fucked you on a beach in Miami. And how beautiful he looked with the ocean framing him as he came.

> *(***VALENTINE*** snaps and the lights go to normal.)*

> *(***BENNY*** decides to do something.)*

YES that's it, think about it baby, think about it. What are we gonna do?

> *(***BENNY*** looks around.)*

A boombox blaring Juan Gabriel?!

Or, we write Alejandro's name in the SKY with SKY WRITING (my favorite type of writing!!)

> *(***BENNY*** grabs a pebble.)*

Or we – oh okay, you're going with that –

"Tap tap on his windowpane". Well you have my blessing and Aretha's, let's do this.

> (**BENNY** *throws the pebble.* **ALEJANDRO** *keeps sleeping.*)

Okay we're gonna pick up another pebble...tap tap on his windowpane –

> (*Another throw.*)

Keep going wake your princess from her SLUMBER.

> (**BENNY** *grabs a bigger rock.*)

OK that one might be a little too...

> (**BENNY** *throws the too-large rock that slams into the window, breaking it.*)

> (**ALEJANDRO** *wakes screaming. He scrambles to the window.*)

> (**VALENTINE** *looks at* **BENNY**.)

...Really?

ALEJANDRO. ...Benny?

BENNY. ...Hi...

ALEJANDRO. WHY DID YOU JUST BREAK MY WINDOW?!

BENNY. It never actually breaks in the movies! I used a little rock and that didn't wake you so I tried a bigger one and I'm sorry.

ALEJANDRO. Why is it that your dumb ass is always trying to traumatizing me in my SLEEP...and why you wearing scrubs?

BENNY. Um...Because...it's a look bitch!...

> (*Slight pause.*)

BENNY. You haven't answered my calls or texts.

ALEJANDRO. I've been busy!

BENNY. With what?

ALEJANDRO. With things –

BENNY. – Things? Things like those three Fire Island-looking tricks you had over tonight?

ALEJANDRO. How long have you been standing there outside?

BENNY. ...Time is a construct, Alejo.

ALEJANDRO.	**VALENTINE.**
BENNY!	Oh Benny...

BENNY. I didn't come here to stalk! I wanted to be fucking romantic with the rock hitting your windowpane –

>   (**ALEJANDRO** *moves to go.*)

Alejo! Please don't go.

>   (**VALENTINE** *snaps and now* **ALEJO** *for a moment is under his spell and in a gold light,* **VALENTINE** *speaks to* **ALEJANDRO**.)

VALENTINE. The way Benny makes up songs and names for each of your plants as he waters them

The way he could always make your Abuela laugh, in her final days, even in broken Spanish.

How hard he dances whenever disco plays.

How once, hiking through canyons in New Mexico, he grabbed your hand and pulled you into the shadows with a grin. And in the darkness, it felt like the canyon itself was teasing, kissing, licking, pushing, opening for you...remember Alejandro and –

>   (*Cupid's gun is heard in the distance.*)

Hurry the fuck up!

(He snaps and **ALEJANDRO** *decides to stay.)*

ALEJANDRO. Fine. What do you want to say?

BENNY. I was hoping…

Meet me tomorrow? Just – please.

Please.

Please?

Por / favor! –

ALEJANDRO. / OK! Okay. Fine. We can meet. Let's meet at the park I go through on my walk to work. Noon.

BENNY. Noon works great…

(Pause as they look at each other.)

ALEJANDRO. Bring glass tomorrow.

BENNY. Glass?

ALEJANDRO. For my window. And take the fucking rock back!

(He throws the rock back down to the street.)

*(***BENNY** *does a little victory dance and walks off past* **VALENTINE.** **ALEJANDRO** *smiling to himself, disappears into the apartment to clean up the broken glass.)*

VALENTINE. Yep totally fine sweetheart, I don't NEED A THANK YOU OR NOTHING.

(He breathes and shakes his muscles out like he just did a work out.)

I feel REFRESHED. That's exactly what I needed. Ya see Cupid! Sometimes it's about leaning into…the work.

(A pause as that gives him an idea.)

VALENTINE. Step two? No that's crazy...

...But I'm very turned on by crazy...

OK, OK, I feel a step two forming –

> *(We hear a loud shot, much closer.* **VALENTINE** *moves to go.)*

(Like the Kool-Aid Man.) OH YEAH!!!

CUPID. *(From offstage.)* VALENTINE!!!!!!!!!!

VALENTINE. *(Like the Kool-Aid Man.)* OH NO.

> *(He disappears.)*

Scene Nine

(Back at the park.)

*(**BENNY** and **ALEJANDRO** sit on the bench.)*

*(**VALENTINE** runs on, sees them.)*

*(**CUPID** runs on after him. **VALENTINE** throws himself to his knees.)*

VALENTINE. Surrender.

*(A pause as **CUPID** stops, breathing hard.)*

CUPID. What?

VALENTINE. I surrender. You got me.

*(A quick pause then **CUPID** shoots him in the knee.)*

FUCKING *communion* I just surrendered!

CUPID. Yeah, well, you dragged me kamikaze-style from space and then had me chasing you all over New Jersey, so I think you deserve some more pain

(Quick pause.)

So? ¡Dale pues pendejo!

VALENTINE. Now?

CUPID. YES! Take me back. Now.

VALENTINE. Alright...But let me just show you –

CUPID. No. Nonono. We're done. This is over. You try and say anything other than up up and away, I shoot your tongue out of your fucking head.

VALENTINE. Can you even do that?

CUPID. You want me to try?

VALENTINE. No I promise it's something you'll want –

IT INVOLVES THAT WOMAN BETTI.

>   *(Silence.)*

CUPID. ...What...

VALENTINE. That tooth fairy-lookin' lady?

CUPID. ...Who...

VALENTINE. Don't try and play *me*, Old Love. I doubled back on you a few times yesterday, and I think you would have definitely been able to catch up to me sooner if you hadn't been spending so much time watching the dental hygienist Becky –

CUPID. *Betti* –

VALENTINE. So you do know her?

>   (**CUPID** *nearly shoots him again in rage. She breathes out.*)

CUPID. I just...

She could see me, and that was interesting, okay? I found it interesting and that's all there is to the whole thing...

VALENTINE. We've met people who could see us. People with the capacity for the Divine. They're rare, but not as rare as Cupid getting a crush on one of them...

CUPID. I. Do. NOT –

VALENTINE. Bullshit. You gave her one of your good kisses. And here I thought you only gave those to me.

CUPID. What, you're jealous?

VALENTINE. PLEASE. Nothing turns me on more than limitless love without edges, and you loving on someone else is music to my parts so nah nah, nah nah nah.

CUPID. *(Flustered)* It's not – she was just...

VALENTINE. Hm?

CUPID. It doesn't matter. This is all EPILOGUE. I don't believe in any of this, hope, humanity, love –

VALENTINE. Not even if I were to tell you about a Great Love (Capital G, Capital L)?

Right here...in New Jersey...

CUPID. There hasn't been a Great Love (Capital G, Capital L) in ages Valentine.

VALENTINE. Jesus you have impossible standards. Romeo and Juliet –

CUPID. Not Great.

VALENTINE. Tristan and Isolde.

CUPID. Not real –

VALENTINE. BATMAN and ROBIN. Very capital G capital L –

CUPID. This is another trick –

VALENTINE. It's really not.

I swear on us. On my love for you.

Give me...five minutes...no tricks...and I can show you a Great Love, Capital G Capital L.

A modern day Batman and Robin, if you will.

(A long beat as they stare.)

CUPID. Fine. You can show me, a quick look...then you take me back and I am officially...

Hasta Luego. ¿Comprendes?

VALENTINE. Si señora. Get in close.

>   (**CUPID** *begrudgingly gets close to him.*)

Hmmm. You smell like fresh laundry.

CUPID. You're not on my good side pendejo. Make with the brujeria.

>   (**VALENTINE** *snaps.*)

>   (*It begins to rain. He pulls out an umbrella for them. And they turn and watch –.*)

>   (*Lights on* **BENNY** *and* **ALEJANDRO** *on the bench.*)

ALEJANDRO. Rain. It's no mystery.

Unlike all this bullshit.

BENNY. You mean you and I?

ALEJANDRO. I was talking about the world at large. You haven't noticed everything going to shit?...But yeah. You and me.

So. I'm here. I came. What do you wanna say?

BENNY. ...That night. Before you left...you said that I hadn't kissed you since January. But I kiss you all the time when you came home from work.

ALEJANDRO. *I* kissed *you* when I came home from work.

BENNY. Or before bed, or whenever you left for the airport, I remember. I remember.

ALEJANDRO. I initiated all those Benny. When I went to Colombia in March? The whole morning I thought, he'll kiss me today. I don't have to be the one to ask for it. I'm about to leave for three weeks, when's the last time we were apart for three weeks?

When I said I was gonna head out you told me to get there safe while you washed the dishes from breakfast. You didn't even look at me Benny...

BENNY. We have sex...

ALEJANDRO. You won't kiss me during sex either. You pulled away from me.

BENNY. I didn't know...

ALEJANDRO. Isn't that worse?

(*Slight beat.*)

Maybe that's okay there's pain right now. Pain can be cleansing and...We ended. We finished. We closed the book.

BENNY. ...We're a book?

ALEJANDRO. Yeah, a book that you're assigned to read in school. Long, tedious, and without a satisfying ending that we'll both learn to live with.

BENNY. ...I'm sorry that my leaving hurt you like that.

ALEJANDRO. Benny I don't want to hear apologies, I wanna hear *why?* Why, straight up?

Don't protect my feelings, don't let my emotions get in the way of you being honest.

I don't care what it is.

You hate my body now? Is that it...?

You got bored.

Really what was it?

You said the words. You left me. Do you really not know why?

(*A beat as* **BENNY** *struggles to find a response.* **ALEJANDRO** *sighs.*)

BENNY. If I could take it back...

ALEJANDRO. You can't.

> (*Silence.*)

> (**ALEJANDRO** *pulls out the photo from Scene Four.*)

The day we met.

Was doing a purge of everything connected to me and you. Couldn't bring myself to get rid of this one. I've been keeping it around with me to...I don't know.

> (*A beat.*)

...Of course I miss you Benny.

BENNY. Could I give you that kiss I should have given you back in March?

> (*They both lean in and kiss.*)

What if I figured out why I said the words? Why I left? Could we...

ALEJANDRO. Benny.

> (**BETTI** *walks on. She's wearing a suit. And looks good.*)

> (*She has a coffee tray with three coffees.*)

BETTI. Hi hi hi. Sorry I don't know what my internal clock is doing lately.

Punctuality is important to me –

VALENTINE. Oh look your girlfriend got the invite...

CUPID. Te *mató* cabrón.

BETTI. (*Continued.*) I asked them to put this weird agave thing in it. Hopefully it's good.

BENNY. Awesome thank you.

BETTI. *(To* **ALEJANDRO.***)* Benny said you'd want a black coffee, no milk, lots of sugar. My Mom used to call this type of coffee "dark as night sweet as sin". You're Alejandro. I'm Betti.

ALEJANDRO. ...Hi?

BETTI. Wow. Benny was right. You're handsome. Your eyes, your hair...should we kiss? No stop we couldn't.

...We shouldn't right?

> *(She glances around...and does she see* **CUPID** *and* **VALENTINE***? The Gods hide behind Valentine's umbrella when they catch her looking.)*

(Confused.) Um – Ignore me. I'm recovering after my DNA being shuffled. Excuse me...

> *(She runs off.)*

> *(A beat as* **ALEJANDRO** *looks at* **BENNY** *in shock.)*

ALEJANDRO. ...WHO THE FUCK WAS THAT?

BENNY. ...Betti.

ALEJANDRO. Are you...seeing someone?

BENNY. ...Not in the conventional sense.

ALEJANDRO. Oh my fucking god. I thought...

What the fuck are we DOING here then?

BENNY. I was lonely, she was lonely, so before you judge –

ALEJANDRO. You're GAY.

BENNY. Sexuality is a SPECTRUM, Alejo.

ALEJANDRO. I'm going to go Benny. I'm going to walk away from you now and I – will...I need to get away from you yep that's what I need to do.

(*He leaves.*)

BENNY. I'm gonna find out why I left I promise!

ALEJANDRO. (*From offstage.*) FUCK OFF.

(**BENNY** *follows.*)

(*A beat as* **CUPID** *looks between where the two lovers were, and* **VALENTINE** *(who looks mortified).*)

(**CUPID** *begins to laugh slowly, the laughter ramping up till she can barely breathe.*)

CUPID. (*Through laughter.*) You're a complete fucking idiot.

VALENTINE. So they are a little rough around the edges...

CUPID. Rough?! These pendejos are TRAIN WRECKS. You think they are a Great Love, Capital ANYTHING?!

(*Continues laughing.*)

VALENTINE. I feel it in my gut, my balls, my halo. They're the real thing!

Let's take them on a Journey. Capital J Journey.

(*A shocked pause from* **CUPID.**)

CUPID. Are you serious? THEM? Journeys – capital Fucking J – are to be given to lovers who deserve it... and even when I was happy go lucky Cupid, shooting people in the ass with arrows...a JOURNEY? We took people on one what...*once* every few centuries? *If* that?

VALENTINE. Then let's do one more. As a goodbye.

One more time. For them and for me and for you.

...One last friendly competition.

(Long pause as she is tempted.)

CUPID. ...Fine.

VALENTINE. *(Overly calm.)* Great.

CUPID. Rules?

VALENTINE. We take them on separate Journeys as far and wide as we can make it. Then bring them together in the end.

CUPID. First one to arrive at the finish line –

VALENTINE. Wins. And holds bragging rights while you go off to your...retirement. Who do you choose?

CUPID. Are you even *trying* to play?! I choose ALEJANDRO. JAJAJAJA you just handed me the game, BITCH. You give me a heartbroken LATINO?!!! PARA MIIIII??? Ay gracias por el regalito chulo, muchisimas gracias.

(She cackles hysterically.)

VALENTINE. Take him. I like Benny, we have history. Plus he is a very confused child. Shit's like vanilla icing to me.

*(**CUPID** kisses La Loca on the tip.)*

(She aims the gun. A red light takes her.)

*(**VALENTINE** crouches and plugs his ears excitedly.)*

Bang Bang!

*(**BENNY** and **ALEJANDRO** appear.)*

*(**CUPID** shoots, and this time her bullets sound like lightning.)*

*(She shoots once – **ALEJANDRO** grabs his chest.)*

*(She shoots again – **BENNY** grabs his chest.)*

*(**CUPID** moves to **ALEJANDRO** and the red light covers them.)*

*(**VALENTINE** to **BENNY**, in a gold light.)*

(The Gods speak to them softly, like lovers.)

CUPID. Keep your heart tight, small, a ball, a speck, a rain drop. Hide it behind layers of blood and fat, keep it bright enough to read by, never bright enough to expose your inner workings to the world.

VALENTINE. Rip your chest open, hard and fast, make it as wide as the sky, show the world your insides, your pain, your joy and welcome them like Noah's Arc, one by one, two by two, into the glass museum of your warm crooked heart

> *(The world shakes and in a flash – the park is now empty.)*

> *(A beat, then **BETTI** comes on.)*

BETTI. Benny and Alejandro, So sorry to keep interrupting but I definitely gave one of you my drink. This one has whole milk. Don't worry it won't kill me, but I drank a third of it before I realized and now I'll be in the bathroom all night and...

> *(Realizing she's alone.)*

Benny?

Hello? Weren't they just here?

I'm really...I'm really losing my grip on reality here...

I feel like a cup under a faucet, a faucet that's been turned to ON since the big bang, I keep feeling *filled*, I'm overflowing with...something –

(She hisses and jerks forward again.)

(She produces another feather.)

(In a terrified whisper.)...Am I turning into a chicken?

(She looks around in fear.)

And now Benny isn't here, and the best part of having him around was not being alone.

(She breathes deep.)

Betti. You are not turning into a chicken.

The faucet is going to turn OFF. Right now!

Starting tomorrow – back. Back! Back to following a script, not living.

No more weird *shit*. Starting...now

(The lights of **THE POET** *flash over* **BETTI**.*)*

(She notices. Stares at the colors on her arms, her hands.)

THE POET. A Rippling – a churning – a foaming – a *birthing*.

*(***THE POET***'s lights disappear.)*

*(***BETTI**, terrified, massages her ears.)*

BETTI. (Who the fuck was that)...

OK. OK. No more weird shit starting – WHAT

(She jerks forward in pain as two beautiful wings erupt from her back.)

(She stares in shock.)

BETTI. Wha...waa...What the fuck was in that MILK?!

ACT TWO

Scene One

(On top of a cliff, in a world made of sky-scratching canyons.)

*(**BENNY** is sleeping surrounded by dirt, dust and sand. He's having a nightmare.)*

BENNY. *(In his sleep.)* You're too much – stop!

(He wakes up, stares in shock and confusion.)

Whatdafuq?!

(He slaps his face.)

Hello? Hello?

(He explores his surroundings, jumps back from the ledge when he sees how high up he is.)

Alejo? AnyBODY?!

*(In a flash of gold – **VALENTINE** appears. He's disguised as an old man in rags.)*

(He speaks in his best old man voice.)

VALENTINE. Well hello there young man –

(**BENNY** *whips around in fear and surprise and his hand lashes out, punching* **VALENTINE** *in the nose.*)

VALENTINE. *(Normal voice.)* The APOSTLES. FUCK.

BENNY. I'm sorry! You surprised me. –

VALENTINE. Oh did I? Did I surprise you Benny?

(*In another gold light, he sheds his disguise, now standing before* **BENNY** *in his normal costume.*)

(**BENNY** *stares in frozen silence.* **VALENTINE** *rubs his nose and glares.*)

You ruined my entrance.

BENNY. I'm sorry?

VALENTINE. I was going to do the wise old man thing. Leading you on your journey with sage wisdom and eventually revealing myself to be me.

BENNY. And...and who are you?

VALENTINE. Oh, right. I am...

(In a grandiose voice.) VALENTINE OF TERNI. THE PATRON SAINT OF LOVE.

(*Gold light surrounds him and trumpets blare as he raises his arms into an epic stance.*)

Nice to meet you / sweetheart.

BENNY. / Your nose is bleeding.

VALENTINE. What? Mother THERESA.

(*Gold light and fanfare stops. He touches his nose.*)

*(Then he bends over and grabs Benny's shirt,
covering his nose with is.)*

(Through the shirt.) This is NOT how the beginning
was supposed to go.

BENNY. I...I don't know what's happening. Or where I am,
or what you're doing and you just did magic –

VALENTINE. I'm a Catholic saint. I don't do magic, I do
miracles.

BENNY. Well good for you. Can you just...

VALENTINE. *(In a dreamy voice.)* All will be revealed my
child.

BENNY. Can you just stop blowing your NOSE ON MY
SHIRT ALREADY.

*(***BENNY*** pushes* ***VALENTINE*** *off.)*

VALENTINE. This is your problem Benny. You push people
away.

BENNY. I'm sorry but what the fuck do you know?

VALENTINE. I know, okay? I am the patron saint of –

BENNY. WHAT DOES THAT EVEN FUCKING MEAN!?

VALENTINE. IT MEANS I KNOW WHAT THE FUCK
I'M TALKING ABOUT! Look you little shitty shit –

BENNY. No YOU look. I'm...somewhere...when a moment
ago I was in a park in Jersey. I don't know what's going
on. So explain to me, who da fuq you are and where da
fuq I am, or I'll punch you again.

(The two glare at each other.)

VALENTINE. ...Alright. I and the God of Love, La Guerrera,
La Luchadora, La Berraca Cupid –

BENNY. Cupid? Little Greek god dude in diapers. Shooting
arrows?

VALENTINE. No that was created to sell shitty chocolate. Cupid is not a he but a she and she's not Greek she's Latina and she upgraded from arrows to bullets at the beginning of the last century...

BENNY. ...*What?*

VALENTINE. DETAILS FOCUS. What's important is that Cupid's a warrior, a gardener, and the garden itself through which love flowers buds blooms...and eventually dies.

BENNY. She...she sounds amazing.

VALENTINE. Yeah. We're all pretty amazing on the Love Team. That's kind of like the best perk of the job...

BENNY. What do you do?

VALENTINE. I assist her in research.

BENNY. ...Research?

VALENTINE. I'm a love scholar. I study breakups, the whys the hows and their impact on the nature of Love as a whole.

BENNY. ...You're the grad student of love?

VALENTINE. It's a little more complex than that –

BENNY. Why does the world need you then? It sounds like Cupid is doing all the work –

VALENTINE. I AM ALSO INTEGRAL! *(Breathes out.)* I am also an important part of the Love Team, 'kay? We're getting way off the fucking agenda.

This is all to say that you, Benny Randle, have been chosen by me. Very important, Saintly, immortal me. For a journey. Spiritual and Physical. Starting here.

> (**VALENTINE** *places his hand on* **BENNY***'s chest.*)

BENNY. My heart? My heart...is a canyon?

VALENTINE. People have a way of building protection around the softest parts of ourselves. That's where we're headed. The softest part of you, Benny.

>　(**VALENTINE** *gently walks forward, forcing* **BENNY** *to take steps to the edge.*)

BENNY. I don't understand –

VALENTINE. Listen if you don't just go with the metaphor of it all, this is gonna be a *long* ass Journey with a Capital J, and time is a'tickin' –

BENNY. Careful – the edge!

>　(**BENNY** *grabs his arm.*)

VALENTINE. I would never hurt you. Trust me.

BENNY. I don't know you.

VALENTINE. I know.

>　(*They look at each other for a moment.*)

>　(**BENNY** *relaxes.*)

BENNY. I'll trust you.

VALENTINE. Thank you. That's a gift.

>　(*He pushes* **BENNY** *over the cliff.*)

>　(*After a moment we hear* **BENNY** *scream.* **VALENTINE** *calls after him.*)

You're doing great sweetie! All part of the process.

>　(*He goes to follow and stops when he hears a sound of clumsy wings.*)

BETTI. AaaaaaaaaAAAAAAAAAAAAAAAAAAAAAAAAAAA AAAAAAA!

>　(**BETTI** *slams into the ground near him.*)

VALENTINE. Betti?!

BETTI. I'm not a chicken!

*(She looks around and sees **VALENTINE**.)*

(Dissapointed.) Oh...you're not...

VALENTINE. Expecting someone else?

BETTI. A little. No offense to you. Today's just been... stressful. And I'm still getting the hang of these –

*(**VALENTINE** gasps **BETTI** yelps.)*

VALENTINE. Her WINGS. Betti you have her wings, you have her wings!!!

BETTI. Whose wings?

*(She screams again in surprise as **VALENTINE** swings her into a happy dance.)*

VALENTINE. I never thought I'd see these two again.

BETTI. Who are you?

VALENTINE. Right, I'm sorry Betti. I'm Valentine, Valentine –

BETTI. *Saint* Valentine, Valentine's Day, that Saint Valentine?

VALENTINE. YES Betti, FINALLY!! How did you end up here?

BETTI. Well, earlier today I was with my faux non-romantic boyfriend slash friend? And I was waiting for him to finish talking to his ex-boyfriend and when I turned back around. They were gone. And these guys popped out of my back and after bringing myself down from a panic attack – I thought maybe there's some kind of chemical in the coffee that...mutated me? So I tried flying over to the local news station so I could let the public know. But these *wings*...do you have any experience in flying?

VALENTINE. Personally no. Though an old love of mine used to take me flying all the time. In the old days. It was always breathtaking.

BETTI. Yeah – no – not for me. It's much harder than you think. A never-ending cardio class.

So I'm flapping above the park like some out of shape drunk pigeon, trying to get some momentum going... but I couldn't concentrate. I kept thinking about...this woman... I met recently. Her name's Cupeeda.

VALENTINE. Aw...Terrible name.

BETTI. So terrible! But her *kiss* was...beauty. It was my...

VALENTINE. First kiss that mattered? And now you feel... reborn...

BETTI. YES! Colors are more vivid...

VALENTINE. You got an incredibly special kiss.

BETTI. OH. Yeah. Like...bro...That kiss took a blowtorch to my life...

I thought about that incredibly special kiss and then suddenly these wings yanked me around and I was surrounded by these lights and then I was falling from up there.

How was my landing. Graceful?

VALENTINE. Oh you know there was definitely an art to it –

BETTI. It was bad.

VALENTINE. – I'm sorry yeah, like a duck shot out of the sky.

BETTI. Mister –

VALENTINE. Oh no no Betti, just Valentine please.

BETTI. Valentine. You're obviously a very important person in the world.

VALENTINE. Oh. Wow. Betti. Thank you, thank you so much. I feel like no one ever *gets* me, and my work, you know –

BETTI. Can you explain what is happening to me? I used to just watch life and I've started to wish I was back there. Watching. All this life I'm living...

I'm really scared.

And you said "her" wings? What does that mean?

> (**VALENTINE** *looks away to where* **BENNY** *fell.*)

VALENTINE. Betti, I think there's someone else you should check in with.

Could I give you a quick blessing?

BETTI. I'm not religious.

VALENTINE. Me either, let's protest at the Vatican when this is all over. But in the meantime...

> (*He kisses her forehead and she's put in a trance, bathed in a gold light.*)

Remember the way she asked you, "Puedo," before her lips touched yours.

Go to her and Give her a message.

> (*He whispers in her ear.*)

> (*He steps back and snaps and* **BETTI** *disappears.*)

> (*He does a little waltz off the cliff after* **BENNY**.)

Scene Two

(In another, nearby, place.)

*(**ALEJANDRO** sits with **CUPID** at the bottom of an ocean.)*

(The world around them is nothing but bright crystal blue water.)

(Mid-conversation:)

ALEJANDRO. Cupid.

CUPID. Hm

ALEJANDRO. The Cupid.

CUPID. La única.

ALEJANDRO. And since when is Cupid a Latina?

CUPID. Did you really think Cupid could be anything but?

(Quick pause.)

*(Then they snicker, **CUPID** giving her hand for **ALEJANDRO** to high five.)*

ALEJANDRO. So now?

CUPID. Well there are some, like Valentine, that believe Capital J Journeys should be intricate things. Long mazes and twists y otra mierda. Pero tu no me pareces alguien que le va a gustar eso.

ALEJANDRO. Para nada.

CUPID. You're honest. You prefer directness.

ALEJANDRO. Completamente.

CUPID. And so, if I were to ask you point blank, what issues you may have with love. Intimacy. With your boyfriend Benny –

ALEJANDRO. *Ex.*

CUPID. ¡Cálmate! With your *Ex*-boyfriend Benny. You would be able to answer me, no?

ALEJANDRO. I guess.

CUPID. So Alejandro Diaz, what are your issues with Love?

ALEJANDRO. Well...none.

> (*Quick silence as she just stares.*)

I *had* them. In the past. Relationships can bring up a lot of...they can be trouble.

But I don't have *issues*. I'm constantly working on myself, physically, mentally, emotionally.

> (*A beat of silence.*)

> (*Eventually* **CUPID** *just smiles and settles down to relax. Maybe she pulls out a pull float and just...floats...*)

...¿y ahora qué?

CUPID. We wait.

ALEJANDRO. Wait for what?

CUPID. For you to stop being a bobo and be honest with me.

> (*She floats in the ocean.*)

> (*He sits, stubborn.*)

ALEJANDRO. Well that's my answer. You can think it's a lie, but that's you. I know myself.

It's a *final* answer. So when you're ready to leave, you let me know.

(She just floats.)

Scene Three

(A child's bedroom. The door of the room is visible and looks dark. And scary.)

(Maybe we see canyons in the distance, through a window.)

*(**BENNY** sits on the bed. He's changed – he looks unwell.)*

*(**VALENTINE** appears in that place. **BENNY** jumps, scared when he enters. He stays quiet while **VALENTINE** looks around.)*

VALENTINE. So this is where we landed huh?

(Silence.)

Do you recognize it? This room?

You built canyons around this place, miles and miles of Earth –

BENNY. Why did you bring me here?

VALENTINE. This is the soft place I was talking about up on the cliff. It looks different for most people but /

BENNY. / But why did you bring me here?

(Quick silence.)

This is my bedroom from when I was a kid. It's not a soft place, it's hard and...can we go? Please, I'd like to go.

VALENTINE. ...We can go.

BENNY. Good.

*(**VALENTINE** goes to the bedroom door.)*

BENNY. Don't!

>   *(He stops.)*

I can't go through there. Can't you just take us out of here without having to go through that...?

VALENTINE. No. Normally I'm all for running away but these soft places are too...sticky...for that. If there's a door here then that's really the only way we –

BENNY. Just stop! Just...

I need a minute.

VALENTINE. ...Take all the time you need.

>   *(He waits.)*

Scene Four

(We go back to **ALEJANDRO** *and* **CUPID**.*)*

(They haven't moved in hours. **ALEJANDRO** *erupts –.)*

ALEJANDRO. OYE!!!! Are we just gonna sit here for the rest of my life?

CUPID. Maybe. I'm willing. I quit my job so I've got no commitments to get to.

ALEJANDRO. You told me this was supposed to be some sort of Journey. We haven't moved in *hours*

CUPID. A journey is a beginning, middle and end cabrón. And you can get to the end without ever taking a step.

(A large sound, muffled in the water, is heard.)

ALEJANDRO. What was that?

CUPID. I have no idea.

(They both look up.)

*(****BETTI*** *lands on the ocean floor.)*

(The wings unfurling behind her like she's some otherworldly angel. Then –.)

BETTI. *(Coughing.)* Water – water. Can't breathe.

CUPID. Betti, breathe, BREATHE, you can breathe this water!

*(****BETTI*** *takes a deep inhale.)*

BETTI. ...Cuepeeda?

ALEJANDRO. ...Cuepeeda?

CUPID. Cállate la boca jetón.

ALEJANDRO. You cállate!

CUPID. What are you doing here?

BETTI. It's an insane story.

> *(The lights of* **THE POET** *land on all three of them.)*

THE POET. My managerial approach to the Universe is a very "hands off" type of style.

The more you futz with a poem – the more you damage it.

But patience is a virtue that this Poet does not possess. So we'll skip ahead...

> *(A snap – everything goes dark.)*

Oh fuck sorry I turned off the Sun. Just a moment –

> *(Another snap and the stage resumes.)*

BETTI. You're Cupid...the god of love?

CUPID. Yeah.

BETTI. Wow...my first real kiss was with a God.

CUPID. Mortals can go haywire with so much...*divinity*. I shouldn't have kissed you / like that.

BETTI. / Don't say that.

I wanted it. Badly.

> *(A beat as they look at each other.)*

> *(***ALEJANDRO*** glares.)*

ALEJANDRO. So do you kiss every person you meet?

> *(They look at him.)*

Benny, Cupid. Gonna try and kiss me again?

BETTI. Oh – um – no thank you Alejandro, this time –

ALEJANDRO. I wasn't –

BETTI. *(Continued.)* I think I'm more you know – lesbian.

ALEJANDRO. I wasn't being serious –

BETTI. Oh! Sarcasm, yeah I know. And if it helps, Benny and I didn't really sleep together. We tried a few times but things didn't quite "fit" –

ALEJANDRO. Let's...not. We don't have to get into that whole "you took my man" riff so...

Nice wings.

BETTI. Thank you so much. But they're not mine. They're yours?

CUPID. They were. Mine haven't been this full and shiny for centuries. I've quit being the God of Love. Ripping these off was my resignation letter. You growing a new set...is the way the Universe is arguing back. Trying to get me to stay.

BETTI. ...You're leaving?

CUPID. Once I finish things with Valentine and this stubborn mocoso –

BETTI. Oh Valentine had a message for you. He said "Almost there. See you at the finish line."

(**CUPID** *freezes.*)

What did he mean by that?

(**CUPID** *whips around and points her shotgun at* **ALEJANDRO**.)

ALEJANDRO. FUCKING / FUCK!

BETTI. / WHAT ARE YOU DOING?

CUPID. You! Make with the revelations and honesty!

ALEJANDRO. What the FUCK –

BETTI. Cupid STOP –

CUPID. This whole thing is supposed to be about the lovers and this isn't a competition. But it's also not NOT a competition. In all the times we've chosen lovers to go on a journey, I have never EVER reached the finish line with my lover after Valentine and his.

I am not leaving this world with him WINNING. TALK. FEELINGS. NOW. No seas tan terco BABOSO!!

BETTI. FOR FUCKS SAKE GIVE HER WHAT SHE WANTS!

ALEJANDRO. I DON'T KNOW I DON'T KNOW

> (**CUPID** *cocks the gun.*)

I – I – DON'T KNOW HOW TO LOVE WITHOUT SHAME OKAY?

> (*A tense pause as she points the gun away.*)

CUPID. Was that so hard?

> (*Beat.*)

> (*She sits down near him.*)

"In your light I learn how to love. In your beauty, how to make poems. You dance inside my chest where no one sees you, but sometimes I do, and that sight becomes this art."

Poem by Rumi. Inspired by his love for Shams. You and Benny remind me of them. A little.

It was always my favorite poem of his.

On the outside I look like the God of Love, La Guerrera, La Luchadora, La Berraca Cupid. A warrior...an ornery, malgeniada, prickly cunt on the outside.

CUPID. But if inside you're this ocean, Alejandro?...I'm Rumi's poem.

En mi núcleo. A person that feels fed by being around others. An extrovert. Una persona que necesita comunidad, familia de sangre, familia echa de experiencias. A friend, a lover, a parent, a stranger, someone's child, someone's abuela, una tía, unos primos, una familia gigante, I have always fucking loved *PEOPLE,* I am the definition of a people person, every day, every day of my long long life... I'm in love with the whole *world*...on the inside...

ALEJANDRO. ...Then why did you quit?

> *(Beat.)*

CUPID. Because I woke up the other day and –

BETTI. Oh you sleep! Good to know. Not that I'm sitting here thinking of you sleeping, or in bed, or in bed with m –

> *(Changes "me" to "moo" when she realizes what she's saying.)*

Mooo...with Moo...a friend of mine. Okay we probably all know I almost said "me" then changed it to "moo" and now I'm mooing over here while we have this big emotional fiesta –

CUPID. *(Nicely.)* Betti...

BETTI. I'm stopping I'll stop.

CUPID. *(To **ALEJANRO**.)* Because I woke up the other day and I realized that I'm really starting to hate people. On the inside. I'm not that poem anymore. I'm just...

Bitter.

And the more I thought that thought...the bitterness welled up like a fucking tsunami. And so I ran...

CUPID. Shams ran from Rumi too. Rumi's disciples harassed Shams to the point he felt he had to disappear, despite his love.

Tu también corriste Alejandro...

(Beat.)

ALEJANDRO. So as a God...do you know things?

CUPID. Some.

ALEJANDRO. My first kiss. You know about that?

CUPID. Raul Botello. You were sixteen.

ALEJANDRO. In my friend Jackie's bed.

CUPID. Drunk on rum.

ALEJANDRO. We were both under the covers.

CUPID. And you were nervous. You'd kissed girls before but this was the first time you had been...

ALEJANDRO. So close to another boy and he smelled...

CUPID. Como licór y la lujuria...

ALEJANDRO. I remember the way he called me papi, before leaning in and...

CUPID. ...fue un beso rico.

ALEJANDRO. Until I ran into the bathroom and threw up. From the rum. And from...

Vergüenza.

Shame is the worst word in English. Doesn't capture anything like the word in Spanish does.

Me siente tan avergonzado, Cupid.

Mi cara se veía mal...

Tiene una cumbia de vergüenza, pisando fuerte por todo mi cuerpo.

ALEJANDRO.   First kisses shouldn't be like that. They should be nothing but joy.

But I grew up. I'm not that boy anymore. I'm not that little boy that thought his type of love was wrong. I'm a man whose loved and has love and…

I thought I outgrew shit. Until the past few months with Benny and it felt like he was pulling away from me and all I could think was that yo, yo estaba hacienda algo mal, it's me it's my fucking body, my fucking face my something, something has changed. So the night we had that fight and Benny brought up breaking up all I could fucking think and feel was this huge tsunami of –

Vergüenza…

But instead of running to the bathroom to throw up I just thought –

Cut all this shit away Alejo, grab scissors bitch, grab a sword, grab an atomic bomb grab *anything* that will get you as far away from this vergüenza as fucking possible. You haven't felt that vergüenza since you were sixteen, you don't have to let it come back.

Pero…nunca se fue…verdad?

CUPID. No…

ALEJANDRO.   …I just want to love. Love on someone, on Benny and just…without feeling bad in the way way back of my mind.

I just want to Love. *(Struggling for words.)* I just wanna –

I just wanna fuck, and love. Like Romeo and Juliet.

I just wanna love sin vergüenza . ¿Cómo puedo hacer eso?

CUPID. Ay, amor.

CUPID. Recoge toda la vergüenza que tienes.

Y escríbele un poema

Un poema con dientes

Y date cuenta de que no es tu vergüenza, sino la del mundo

> *(Beat.)*

And show Benny your burden.

Stop running.

ALEJANDRO. Bueno...

> (**CUPID** *snaps and in a red flash.*)

> (**ALEJANDRO** *disappears.*)

BETTI. ...Wow...

CUPID. Hm...

BETTI. You're incredible.

CUPID. *(Shy.)* Oh...thank you. It's just...whatever. It's my job. *Was* my job...

BETTI. You're nicer thank you think.

CUPID. No I'm mean and dead inside.

> (**BETTI** *laughs.*)

BETTI. So what do we do now?

> *(For a moment they might kiss. Then* **BETTI** *chickens out...)*

CUPID. Follow him to the finish line. Do you mind...giving me a ride?

BETTI. Of course not. But he just disappeared. How do we follow...

CUPID. It's all metaphor. Just fly up and we'll get there.

(**BETTI** *offers her hand.*)

(*After a beat.* **CUPID** *takes it.*)

(*They begin to fly.*)

BETTI. So...am I becoming...like...a god...like you? Or a Saint like Valentine?

CUPID. Do you wanna be any of that?

BETTI. Well...the only experience I have with playing God is when I play the Sims...

I have no idea what kind of god I would be. Would I be like "Saint Betti, Goddess of...loneliness, and oral hygiene? I'm not anything special...

CUPID. I think you're special...

BETTI. Special people can't say that. And you're like...a nuclear weapon level of Special.

And I have to be honest, Cupid, I don't know if this level of Special is...healthy...for me...

CUPID. ...Do you want me to take the wings back?

BETTI. Can you?

CUPID. I don't want to...but if you want to go back to your life...I will

(*A few beats.*)

BETTI. So...you know things about people's lives?

CUPID. Some things. Perks of the job. I know a lot of things like first kisses, first loves...lots of firsts.

BETTI. Do you know things about...parents? Like...my parents? Just as an example...

CUPID. Sure yeah.

BETTI. *(Nonchalantly.)* Interesting, interesting.

> *(A beat.)*

> *(The lights have shifted, the world speeding by them in bright flashes.)*

BETTI. Did they...so there was no love between them, right?

CUPID. Is that what they told you?

BETTI. Yes! They said they were only together for the papers.

CUPID. Liars. That was part of it sure but trust me, at one point they were all fireworks and making love all the time and...

BETTI. *(In surprise.)* Really?!

> *(She throws her hands in the air in excitement.)*

OH MY GOD. And here I always thought that they were just – I thought I couldn't ever be in love because I wasn't...that's INCREDIBLE that's –

> *(She realizes she has dropped **CUPID** who is now falling, screaming.)*

Oh fuck. I got you!

> *(She dives after her.)*

Scene Five

(Back in Benny's childhood bedroom.)

(A beat of silence.)

*(**BENNY** is now curled up in bed, away from the door and facing away from **VALENTINE**.)*

VALENTINE. Benny – how we doing?

(Quick silence.)

This is where you grew up, hm?

This place feels like more than a bedroom. It's part place, part memory. Colored with how a child experiences things. All raw emotion without the tools to process it.

Benny. Did something happen here?

*(A pause then **BENNY** sits up.)*

BENNY. Do you have experience with pain, Valentine?

VALENTINE. I've had my fair share.

BENNY. Me too. Before Alejo...I felt like I met no one but Pain. First kiss? Pain. Motherfucker bit me.

VALENTINE. Trying to be sexy?

BENNY. Trying. Made my lip bleed. The first time I had sex? Wooooo.

VALENTINE. Painful?

BENNY. Very. I was eighteen, meeting a guy off Craigslist, not knowing *anything* about gay sex. Tried bottoming with no lube.

I'm telling you. First relationships with men were all Pain.

BENNY. Pain took me out on a date then didn't call me after fucking.

Pain saw insecurity under the sass and ran like Road Runner whoosh, beep beep.

Pain kissed me at night, then called me a faggot at school during the day.

Pain Pain Pain Pain Pain.

VALENTINE. ...And was there pain here? In this room?

(A beat.)

BENNY. Pain touched me when I was nine.

It happened continuously for about a year and a half. I didn't know what was happening, not really.

During the day I was distracted by school and friends around the neighborhood, games with my siblings. But whenever my Mom would settle me in bed for the night I would...

In the darkness of this room I couldn't run from the thoughts...

I swear I don't think I slept once during that time. All I remember is staring at this door, wishing I could walk through it and tell my mother what was happening. I'd sometimes make it all the way down the hall, to her door. But I couldn't ever bring myself to knock.

And eventually I couldn't even get near the door. Would wet the bed if I had to go to the bathroom instead of getting up and...

(He gets up from the bed.)

I always thought that when I met the right guy...he would be able to take this room. That door...Scoop it out. Make me whole

VALENTINE. It's not like that at all.

BENNY. I think it's harder to deal with the dark corners of your mind when you're in love. The light of it, good healthy love, is bright. Shines a light on everything you've packed away. No shadows left to hide anything in.

(He gets up from the bed and paces.)

Back in January, Alejandro and I went out for drinks with some friends and family. We came back, tried to have sex, were way too tired and just went to bed instead.

And in the middle of the night we woke up because...I had wet the bed.

We laughed, cleaned up, turned the mattress over and went back to sleep. Well Alejo went back to sleep. But I...

Was here. But instead of my mom down the hall I had Alejandro right there laying next to me and...

VALENTINE. You didn't tell him?

BENNY. No, I just started getting resentful, picking fights, arguing about dumb shit, trying to make up excuse after excuse why I didn't want to go to bed yet...mad that he wasn't magically making things better. That he wasn't the prince coming in and slaying the dragon of this room...

VALENTINE. Maybe he can...Or maybe he'll craft *you* a sword to do the slaying.

Or he'll turn the dragon into a pool for you to play in.

Or maybe he'll learn how to hold you...in moments when you feel like you're in back here in this room.

Reminding you that you're safe in your body.

You're safe with him.

And...you're safe with me.

*(**VALENTINE** gets up.)*

VALENTINE.   Fuck it. Go through the door, don't go through the door. I'll fight our way out of here. Cupid was always the warrior between us but...I can be more of the warrior for you in this moment. I'll rip our way out of here. I'll Kool-Aid Man punch my way through these walls and a hundred others after, if it means you don't have to do something you don't want to do.

(A long beat.)

BENNY. I want to.

(He goes to the door and goes through.)

(The soft places fade...)

Scene Six

*(We see **BENNY** standing alone in the middle of his and Alejandro's bedroom. He stands unsure for a moment.)*

(Then we hear a grunt and we see the bed in the corner of the room lift for a moment as if pushed from below.)

*(**ALEJANDRO** crawls out from under the bed, breathing hard, and confused.)*

ALEJANDRO. Why the fuck did I come out from under the bed?

(A beat.)

(The magic, the Journey, all the impossible evaporates.)

(And it's just the two of them. Looking at each other.)

It's you.

BENNY. Me. You?

ALEJANDRO. Me.

(They walk to each other.)

(For a beat their hands touch – as if to make sure they're real.)

ALEJANDRO & BENNY. *(Relief.)* You.

(They hug.)

*(With a crash **CUPID** barrels through as if through the window.)*

*(At the same moment, **VALENTINE** appears in a gold flash.)*

BENNY.
AHHH!

ALEJANDRO.
My window!

CUPID & VALENTINE. I WIN! The FUCK you do!

CUPID. You teleported here I managed to get here before you *without* wings / so I deserve the win on that alone. YOU TELEPORTED – ay por favor – YOU'RE A SORE LOSER who just can't stand

VALENTINE. / So what it's not like you took a greyhound. I won. No no NO my feet touched the ground before – you ALWAYS do this, this is just like what happened in Russia in early – no, you pull /

(They're argument is cut off by:)

BENNY.
STOP!

ALEJANDRO.
¡CÁLLENSE!

*(A quick pause as **CUPID** and **VALENTINE** stop.)*

CUPID.
We'll talk about this later, yeah that's fine.

VALENTINE.
We don't have to – yeah that sounds good.

(An awkward moment as they all look at each other, seeing who will go first...)

ALEJANDRO. *(To **VALENTINE**.)* I'm Alejandro Camilo María Diaz.

VALENTINE. Saint Valentine of Terni.

CUPID. *(To **BENNY**.)* Cupid, God of Love (retired).

BENNY. I'm Benny...from Hackensack...

(A quick pause then all at once.)

ALEJANDRO. *(To* **CUPID.***)*

Muchas gracias por todo –

CUPID.

Claro chulo, con gusto –

BENNY. *(To* **VALENTINE.***)*

It was beautiful working with you –

VALENTINE.

Thank you babe, what a lovely home, I've only seen it from the fire escape...

(Slight pause then a bump from the closet. **BENNY** *opens it.)*

BETTI. And I'm Betti! The dental hygienist.

*(***ALEJANDRO*** opens the closet.)*

*(***BETTI*** comes falling out.)*

BETTI. ...I'm late.

CUPID. No! No. Well...

BETTI. Dammit. Wait, Cupid, we were flying up and then...

ALEJANDRO. We all came from different directions...

BETTI. How?

VALENTINE. It's a metaphor.

BETTI. Oh...

*(***BETTI*** and ***BENNY*** go to each other.)*

Oh Benny you're giving me another first. My first break up!

BENNY. Yeah Betti, and you're giving me my first time... seeing...a person...with wings...

Oh my god you have wings...

Honestly...

They work on you.

BETTI. Benny, you're beautiful.

BENNY. You're divine...

BETTI. Literally! I have wings now!

I wish every person who came in for a teeth cleaning led me to completely smashing myself down into a seed and then growing in to be the flying dental hygienist lesbian kisser that I am right now. Thank you for the newness and the attempts at (Sorry Alejo) sex.

And even if I live long enough to watch the Sun go boom...I'll remember the way you lied with me naked by a river in Jersey. And made me feel seen.

I hope all my future ex-lovers are as amazing as you.

> (*She takes* **BENNY** *and* **ALEJANDRO**'*s hands and puts them together.*)

> (*She then smacks their butts then stands to the side of* **CUPID** *and* **VALENTINE**.)

ALEJANDRO. So...

BENNY. How do these Journeys end?

> (**CUPID** *and* **VALENTINE** *look at each other. They both snap. The room goes red and gold.* **VALENTINE** *goes to* **BENNY**. **CUPID** *to* **ALEJANDRO**.)

> (*In simultaneous movement, they kiss the lovers. First on the forehead. Then their eyelids.*)

> (*And finally, the kiss them on the mouths. Deeply. They pull back and whisper.*)

CUPID.	VALENTINE.
Bendito sea, bendito sea, bendito sea tu Corazón lleno de suave lluvia y relámpagos a la vez.	Blessed Be, Blessed Be, blessed be your heart filled with soft rain and lightning all at once.

(The Gods disappear.)

(A beat then.)

(ALEJANDRO *starts taking off his clothes.)*

BENNY. Alejo what are you –

ALEJANDRO. Turn on all the lights.

BENNY. But daylights out.

ALEJANDRO. Doesn't matter. We need every light in here turned on. I mean everything. Get every electronic device and and and...all screens should be set on full brightness. Go.

(A moment – then **BENNY** *does this.)*

(ALEJANDRO *strips slowly down to his underwear.)*

(BENNY *finishes turning everything on.)*

BENNY. That good?

ALEJANDRO. Yeah. Now take off your clothes. Please.

(A pause, then **BENNY** *complies.)*

(They look at each other.)

ALEJANDRO. I want to tell you some things. Some things about me. About us too, but mostly...

BENNY. Alejo...

ALEJANDRO. I want to have the conversation we should have had that night. The night we broke up.

I want to tell you things. Things I've never told a partner. Things I'm afraid of letting roll out of my head and down my tongue and out my mouth. Things that never made it past my lips.

Cause Benny, you, you, I fucking love.

BENNY. Alejo –

ALEJANDRO. No Benny, let me talk first, let me talk... I need to talk for a while and it could be all I need to say are just a few words or – or, it could be that I need to talk for a few days straight. And maybe, after all the talking. We can just...Go to bed –

BENNY. Yes, but Alejo –

ALEJANDRO. We can take the rest of this off each other then lie naked wrapped up in the sheets just me and you in our own little world...and talk this shit out...

Cause I want to show you everything papi. I want to be completely honest with you con nada bloquenado tu y yo Benny, Quiero hablar y quiero perderme en ti como un cañón – yo te amo Benny, Te amo con –

> (**BENNY** *has walked over and gently covered* **ALEJANDRO***'s mouth with his hand.*)

BENNY. I'm gonna let you talk. And you can talk for a few minutes, or a hundred years. I'm going to listen. To all of it. I'll even take notes. Copious notes. I'll take in all the things you need to say and listen to it all, hard. And then yeah...going to bed sounds perfect...

Cause I love you too.

But, before you do that. I need to talk about something that happened to me.

> *(He moves his hand.)*

ALEJANDRO. Okay.

BENNY. Okay.

> *(Quick beat.)*

When I was nine...

> *(After a moment, **ALEJO** puts his hand on **BENNY**'s cheek. **BENNY** grabs his hand and keeps it there.)*

Scene Seven

(**BETTI**, **CUPID** and **VALENTINE** are on Cupid's asteroid.)

(They have all been watching The Lovers. **CUPID** is weeping.)

VALENTINE. You always did the heavy lifting when it comes to Love.

Everything I know, I learned from you.

One of the first things I can remember learning from you was that, that right there?

(He points down to the world below. To **BENNY** and **ALEJANDRO**.)

Is what great love is. Not some epic romance. It's simple. Painful. Joyous. Something you work at. There is no Great Love, Capital G, Capital L. It's just love. And it can't change the world. And it can't make all the bad go away...but it helps. Like balm to an open wound. It helps.

(**CUPID** turns around to the door she made at the beginning.)

So. Full circle. I told you I would let you go as soon as we blessed them so...Ta da. You can go now.

(A pause.)

CUPID. I'm a woman of my word.

VALENTINE. Yes.

CUPID. So I'm going to go. But...I'll come back.

VALENTINE. Yeah?

CUPID. Yeah. I think I will. But I'm taking a break, I fucking deserve one, okay?

VALENTINE. You do, you very much do.

CUPID. But...write me letters? While I'm away. I miss your letters... I'll miss you.

VALENTINE. I'll write you one every day. Even if I'll miss you more than words can –

>*(She pulls him in close and kisses him.)*

Old Love.

CUPID. Old Love.

>*(She looks over at* **BETTI**.*)*

Betti? Are you ready? I'll take back those wings...

BETTI. Yeah...well...um...I never really felt human, anyways.

I don't know what kind of deity I'll be...But these wings now feel like a birthmark.

I like being Betti with wings.

...I like Betti.

So whatever god I become...it will look like Betti with wings.

As long as you're still okay with...

CUPID. Keep them. They look better on you anyway.

>*(A quick beat.)*

Why don't you come? I could use company.

BETTI. What's on the other side?

CUPID. ...Well I had originally planned to go to a world filled with nothing but night and silence...

CUPID. But I don't know. I haven't taken a break in a long time and...I just want to lie down somewhere new.

BETTI. ...Those worlds in Alejandro and Benny. The ocean, the canyons...

Do I have something like that? Inside?

(**CUPID** *nods and* **BETTI** *thinks.*)

Can we go to my place? My little world.

CUPID. What do you think it looks like?

BETTI. What does Betti look like on the inside?

Like...the inner script I lived by for so long? But the script has been blown apart from the inside. And burned to ashes.

But the ashes are being lifted by this wind, a wind that sometimes sounds like my laugh, and sometimes sounds like my scream. The wind is shaping the ashes into giant monuments of monsters and gods and rivers and wings and...dental offices are outlawed in this world...

It's an insane alien place that only I would love...

But maybe you'll enjoy exploring it with me?

CUPID. ...That sounds like a really fun date.

BETTI. OH thank god, I had no idea what I was saying and I was planning on throwing myself off this rock if you rejected me...

...Before we go...I've been flapping through multiple worlds and magic and pain to get the chance to do this again...

(*She quickly goes to* **CUPID** *and kisses her.* **CUPID** *goes a lil limp.*)

(**VALENTINE** *does a happy little clap. Then* **CUPID** *goes and hands him La Loca.*)

CUPID. You'll wait?

VALENTINE. *(He takes the gun.)* I'll be here.

(*With a last wave,* **CUPID** *opens the door. And she and* **BETTI** *go through.*)

(**VALENTINE**, *looks around.*)

(*He takes a seat. Pulls out some binoculars from his pocket.*)

While we wait, let's take a closer look at how the Benny and Alejandro reunion is going.

(*He looks.*)

(*Slowly, the lights of* **THE POET** *appear all over the stage, growing through the following.*)

Oh shit. Bow chica wow wow.

… I shouldn't be watching this.

(**THE POET** *is heard.*)

THE POET. But Valentine keeps watching.

And below the heavens, in Hackensack NJ, our lovers have finished talking, finished pouring our their secrets and pain. And now in the aftermath of all that truth, they are doing what Lovers do best.

(*In the bed on Earth,* **ALEJANDRO** *and* **BENNY** *are wrapped around each other, the covers hugging them as they move.*)

They fumble at times. Remembering each other's bodies.

THE POET.   They whisper words of safety, words so beautiful that this Poet dares not repeat them. It would ruin it.

So let's just watch. Watch Benny and Alejandro make love in the most honest way they can.

And it's not the hottest thing you'll ever see.

And it's not something they would depict in an epic romance.

And it's not how Romeo fucked Juliet. It's just real.

And my word...

Isn't that the most fabulous poetry?

Un poema fabuloso.

End of Play

Printed in the USA
CPSIA information can be obtained
at www.ICGtesting.com
LVHW010230110224
771451LV00003B/347